RONAN & JULIETTE

Jenny Taylor

Table of Contents

Chapter 1

Juliette

JULIETTE MONTE NEEDED A BREATHER. Just a moment alone to *think*. Between her best friend Lois's incessant chatter and the constant, overbearing presence of her boyfriend she felt suffocated. It didn't help that her classmates were now surrounding her like a thick mob of grumbling bullfrogs. This field trip was a bit too much after a chaotic week at school. Her senior class had already spent four hours hiking through the damp trails of Hudson Valley, New York, and everyone was exhausted and grouchy. Dark clouds had been threatening rain throughout the day, making the air dense and filling the forest with the heavy scent of pine.

"Listen up kids," Mr. Seymour shouted, using his 'outside' voice, "we've still got an hour until this bus gets here, and I'm out of ideas on how to keep you all from getting on my last nerve. So, let's make the most of it! Good old-fashioned hide-and-seek."

Loud groans could be heard throughout the crowd. "Do we have to?" moaned one of Juliette's classmates.

"Yes," Mr. Seymour replied firmly. "This is mandatory. Stay close enough to hear my whistle. When you hear it, it's time to go home. Do *not* make me go searching for you. Philip Bryans! You are going to start. On the count of three, everyone run and hide!" Mr. Seymour was obviously more excited about this game than his students.

Juliette, however, was thrilled. Hiding was exactly what she wanted to do. Her boyfriend, Todd, had been especially moody today. He could be quite brooding on a normal day, but he barely said three words to her all afternoon. There was, as far as she could tell, no reason for him to be so melancholy. She had analyzed every conversation they'd had in the previous week, and determined it probably had nothing to do with her. Her head ached from the mental gymnastics as much as her calves from the endless walking.

Juliette spotted a deer stand and made a run for it as soon as Philip Bryans started counting. Todd wouldn't expect it, and there was no way that Lois could keep up with her. Juliette wasn't an athlete, but Lois was opposed to running for any reason, other than perhaps being chased by a bear. "Boys like thick girls," Lois would tease; no doubt to soothe herself for being considerably larger than Juliette. Juliette planned to relax up there and read her old, worn copy of *Catcher in the Rye*, which she'd rolled up in her oversized yellow raincoat. She reached the deer stand so fast that she could barely hear Lois yelling "Hey, wait!"

Not a chance, Lois, Juliette thought as she smiled to herself in satisfaction. *Todd probably doesn't even realize he's been abandoned.*

Just a few more steps and she could relax.

Instead of peace, she faced the bitter disappointment of Ronan Richland's beautiful, smirking face. He was sprawled across the seat of the deer stand, like Adonis waiting for his Aphrodite. He was the type of good-looking that made every girl do a double take; tall, dark, and handsome with insatiable dimples and chiseled muscles. Unfortunately, his reputation as a lady killer was notorious.

"What? Why are you here! This was my spot!"

5

"Not a chance. I got here first, and I'm not moving." He laced his fingers in satisfaction and placed them behind his head. The shaky wooden deer stand was only meant to seat two people, and with his long legs propped up, he was taking up nearly all the room there was.

She had known Ronan for as long as she could remember, but she kept her distance. Juliette knew she was not immune to Ronan's dangerous good looks.

She considered turning around, but soon heard their classmates' voices drawing in below them. She shuddered at the thought of being in the midst of that swarm again. "There's no way I'm leaving."

"Look, Princess, there are a thousand little hideouts in these woods. I'm not leaving. First come, first serve."

Juliette could hear Lois attempting to softly call her name, which was impossible with her loud, booming voice. She cringed. She loved Lois, honestly, but her constant chatter was hard for her mind to keep up with.

Ronan chuckled. "Sounds like someone's looking for you."

"Ronan, please. I'm begging you." She did her best to look pitiful.

Ronan peered over the edge of the lookout. "Here comes your lame boyfriend. I guess you want him up here too. Shall I call him for you?"

Juliette leapt forward and threw her hand over Ronan's mouth. "Don't you dare," she seethed. Many girls, and guys for that matter, would be afraid of a confrontation with Ronan Richland, but Juliette knew he was harmless. Their parents had been friends when they were second graders, so she frequently had dinner at his house. She taught him to tie his shoes, they built Lego mansions together, and she had even seen him cry while watching the Lion King. He had become a pretty severe bully during his middle school years,

6

but Juliette had never been his victim. There was an unspoken understanding that she was not someone he would mess with.

Ronan's smooth lips curled, and his eyes sparkled with amusement. This only served to irritate her more. "So you don't want Todd up here with you? Interesting. Wouldn't this be the perfect spot for you guys to make out? What's the problem, Princess?"

Juliette glared at him.

"He's gay, isn't he? I knew it."

"How dare you? He is not! Not every relationship is just physical, Ronan. Ours is deeper than that. Not that I would expect you to understand," Juliette hissed, doing her best to be intimidating without drawing the attention from anyone below them.

Ronan rolled his eyes and crossed his arms. "Yeah right, Juliette. That dude is not interested in you. It's pretty obvious that you're not into him either. I don't think I've ever even seen you guys touch." He leaned forward, flashing his movie star smile. "I'd bet my car that he's never even kissed you."

Juliette narrowed her eyes. She would not back down to this boy. "Like I would tell you!"

Ronan's smile grew, as if he was enjoying this exchange. "Oh my God! You've never kissed anyone. How cute are you?"

She gasped.

Could he be any ruder?

"Of course I have," she said matter-of-factly. Jake Williams had kissed her behind the church in seventh grade, and she had run away crying. She cringed internally at the memory of his braces scraping against her lips. A kiss was a kiss though.

Ronan leaned back again and laughed softly. "What a load. Aw, you are just too precious, Jewels. I wouldn't expect anything less from you."

Her body temperature began to rise. She wanted to shed her raincoat, despite the chill in the air. "I'm an amazing kisser. Too bad you'll never know."

"Prove it."

"Excuse me?"

Ronan shrugged, leaned forward, and casually repeated, "Prove it. I dare you."

Juliette glared in disbelief.

"That's what I thought," Ronan said smugly.

"I have a *boyfriend,* Ronan."

Ronan rolled his eyes. "Psh, please. As if I'm interested. And you barely have a boyfriend. More like a girlfriend."

"Todd is smart, and mature, and he respects me. He doesn't view women as some type of conquest for personal pleasure," she retorted.

"I should have known you would turn this into a lecture." He leaned back and pulled his hood over his head. "You can sit on the other side, Jewels. Wake me up when it's time to go."

He's treating me like a freaking kid! And how dare he call me "Jewels?" No one has called me that since middle school!

She thought about the many girls that usually surrounded him at school. He seemed to gravitate towards the tall, curvy ones in particular. She suddenly felt rather small and vulnerable in her large raincoat that covered her own soft curves. She needed to prove herself.

"Okay, fine." Juliette stood a little taller. "I'll kiss you."

Ronan chuckled. She placed her hands on her hips firmly and refused to break her stare. Ronan raised his eyebrows. "Oh, you're serious?" He threw his hood back and leaned forward. "Alright, Monte. Show me what you got."

Juliette closed her eyes and cleared her mind. Lois had told her that when she finally kissed Todd, all she had to do was "Put your whole self into it, everything you've got. Hold nothing back."

Ronan gingerly rose to his feet, muttering, "I can't wait to see this…"

Juliette stepped up, grabbed his hoodie, and pulled him in. She put her whole heart, soul, her entire being into this moment, making Ronan her practice pillow. She was not expecting the flood of emotions that encompassed her. After a few moments, he wrapped his arms around her petite waist and pulled her closer. And closer. And closer. Until she could feel his heart beating furiously against her chest, and she felt like she might melt through the floorboards. Every nerve in her body was responding to his touch. He was strong and warm, he tasted like mint and smelled like bergamot and citrus. It felt completely natural. She would never know how long they stood in that moment; time seemed to stand still.

Heavy rain began pounding against the tin roof of the deer stand as she slowly pulled away and found herself staring straight into Ronan's eyes. She wished she could read his thoughts, but she couldn't even decipher her own. Perhaps he felt as she did; overwhelmed. His shaky breathing gave her the impression that she had proved herself worthy after all.

A loud whistle snapped them back into reality. Juliette realized she was clutching Ronan's hoodie, while his arms were still tightly wrapped around her waist. They dropped their hands simultaneously as if awakened to the strangeness of this situation.

Juliette slowly backed up to the ladder of the deer stand, her eyes still locked with Ronan's. With a quick breath, she pulled her yellow hood up, and clambered down the ladder as if she was being chased. She ran so fast back to the bus that the hood of her raincoat fell back, soaking her wispy blonde hair to her head. The cold water felt good. Her skin was on fire. Once she was on the bus, she staggered to her seat next to Lois.

"You poor thing! You look like a drowned cat. I couldn't find you anywhere! Where'd you go?"

"Oh ... I found a great spot..." Juliette couldn't look her in the eye. She wasn't good at hiding her emotions, and Lois was great at reading her every thought. She pulled her backpack into her lap and buried her face in it, looking for anything to dry her hair.

Ronan jumped up the steps of the bus and paused, looking directly at her. He was breathing heavily and his cheeks were bright red. He quickly glanced at Lois, who was obliviously chatting away, then turned back to Juliette and they stared at each other, bewildered.

"Step on it, Richland!" Came a voice from behind him. "We're getting soaked!"

He stumbled past Juliette, briefly pausing. Panic arose in Juliette's throat as he opened his mouth, then instant relief as he slowly put his earbuds in and took his seat in the back of the bus.

Lois chattered the entire two-hour drive back to the school, blissfully unaware that her best friend was slowly unraveling next to her. Juliette would occasionally respond with a "yeah" or "huh," but her thoughts were spinning faster than she could process.

You kissed Ronan Richland. That just happened.

She tried putting the euphoria of that kiss out of her mind. No wonder he always had girls fighting over him. With those smooth muscles and luscious lips... *Stop it, Juliette! What are you thinking?* She was better than all those other girls at school, right? She couldn't believe that she was the type of person to cheat on her boyfriend, especially with someone like Ronan. Was it cheating, though? She tried rationalizing her actions to soothe her conscience.

It was just a dare. Just a dare. It didn't mean anything.

She suddenly had the sick realization that he would probably tell people about this. He was probably texting everyone at this moment - "Hey you know that prude, Juliette Monte? She made out with me on our field trip."

No, no, no, no, no!

Juliette turned only once to look at Ronan, who was tucked in the back with his hood up, looking at his phone.

If I had his number I could text him and beg for mercy. I wonder how I can get it...

Her eyes then met Todd's, who gave her a sweet smile.

Of course, now you want to be a nice boyfriend. She smiled back weakly. *What if Ronan is texting Todd right at this moment? Oh, I feel sick.*

It was dark when they finally reached the school and Lois drove her home.

"You sure you don't want to spend the night?" Lois asked as she pulled into Juliette's driveway. "We can stay up all night talking!"

For the love of God, no.

"I'm super tired... maybe tomorrow?" She asked with another weak smile. "I really just want to go to bed."

"Sure thing! Get yourself a hot shower and a cup of tea. Nighty-night!"

11

"See ya!" Juliette waved, then quickly walked through the drizzling rain. She shut the front door, leaned against it and took deep, ragged breaths in and out through pursed lips. It didn't help.

"Hey! You hungry?" Her mom called from the kitchen. "I made pot roast."

"No, I ate. I'm really tired, so I'm going to bed."

Juliette ran up the stairs to her room before her mother could respond. She could not face her mother tonight, and she needed to formulate a plan to prevent the complete destruction of her reputation. She shut her door, flung herself on the bed and covered her face, trying to disappear.

What just happened?

Chapter 2

Ronan

RONAN COULDN'T SLEEP AT ALL THAT NIGHT. The rain continued on and off all Friday night and into Saturday, so he didn't feel guilty about staying in bed. He didn't feel like going out in this frame of mind anyway. Staying home was unusual for him. He would typically go out as much as possible and keep himself busy. The looming sadness in his house was overwhelming, so the less time he had to spend in it, the better.

He restlessly glanced over at his alarm clock at 10am.

"Screw this," he muttered to himself and grabbed his phone, surrendering to his curiosity. He spent the next few hours stalking Juliette Monte on every possible social media outlet. She was just as he'd always imagined. Sweet, innocent, pure. On any other day this would have seemed boring to him, but today he was fascinated.

He let out an exasperated sigh as he scrolled through her short Instagram page.

What kind of girl doesn't have a single selfie on her profile page? What is up with this chick?

Most of the pictures he could find were ones that she had been tagged in with her family, or church events that she had been part of.

Ronan and Juliette had attended the same church up until 5th grade, when his parents died. He still recognized many of the faces in her pictures. There were people there that had been like family to him. His chest tightened as he looked at them feeding the homeless and going on "missions" trips. Ironically, they had been strangely absent when his life spiraled out of control, and he lived ten streets away.

When he came upon a picture of Juliette at homecoming earlier that year, he stopped scrolling. Her glowing smile radiated through his screen. Her picture seemed to come alive, a glimmering paradox in his gloomy room. Everything around him dulled in comparison. She had on a short lilac lace dress that perfectly hugged her subtle curves. She had big, deep brown eyes that seemed to be looking straight into his soul. And those lips. He shuddered and bit his thumb, trying to rouse himself.

I must be losing it, he thought.

Ronan had more than a dozen girls that he could probably call for a hook-up, but that kiss was like a drug. As much as had tried to shake it off, he knew he had never experienced anything quite like it. Little Juliette, who seemed so sweet and pure, was some kind of sexy goddess in reality. Up to this point, kissing had always just been a means to get a girl to give him what he really wanted. It was as if

14

Juliette had pulled at some string that was deep within his soul. He couldn't focus on anything else. That kiss felt like something more, a connection he couldn't quite pinpoint, and it was driving him nuts. Whatever it was, he needed more.

He moved on to Todd's page and scrolled through pictures of Juliette and Todd together. They always seemed to be at arm's length, even at school. Todd was proper and serious, with thick-rimmed glasses and his dark hair slicked back to his head. Ronan wanted to jump in that picture and ruffle his hair up.

Nerd, he thought spitefully.

Ronan wondered if Todd was dating Juliette to end the constant teasing he had received in junior high about being gay. Ronan had been guilty of some of that teasing, but he hadn't messed with Todd in the last few years.

It had surprised Ronan when Todd and Juliette became a couple. He remembered what Juliette said the day before, "Not every relationship is just physical, Ronan. Ours is deeper than that." He scoffed to himself.

What does that even mean?

He groaned loudly and buried his face in his pillow.

There was a loud knock on his door "You okay in there? You sick or something?" His older brother, Mike, asked.

As if he cares. "I'm fine."

15

"Okay, I ordered a pizza if you want some dinner."

Dinner? "What time is it?"

"5:30."

So I spent the whole day stalking Juliette online? What kind of a loser-

"And Samantha is here."

Ronan smiled.

Samantha! Perfect distraction. He swung his bedroom door open.

"'Sup, boo," Samantha purred. She was a stocky redhead with big green eyes outlined in thick black eyeliner. She had been in love with him for years, and he had taken full advantage of it. He had tried hard this past year to clean up his reputation as a party animal and playboy, but he occasionally indulged in the all too willing Samantha.

"Come in," Ronan grinned.

"I was in the neighborhood so I thought I'd pop in and see what you are up to."

As if they didn't both know why she was here. She took her jacket off to reveal a tank top that was painfully small and tight. The smell of her musky perfume punched him in the senses as soon as she stepped forward. She didn't waste any time, but leaned in and started kissing him aggressively. He wrapped his arms around her, willing himself to be turned on, but this was no Juliette-kiss. She shoved her tongue deep into his mouth. The taste of her lip balm turned his stomach and acid bit the back of this throat. He attempted to kiss her back, but quickly realized it was not happening today. It felt cheap and rushed. It was robbing him of the glow he was still relishing from Juliette. She moved to his neck and started fidgeting with his belt.

I need to get out of this quick, he thought as he searched his mind for a way to gently let her down.

"Hey listen, I'm not feeling good. I think I better go back to bed."

Samantha stared at him, stunned. Her pale, freckled face turned bright red. Rejecting a casual hook up was new territory for him, and Samantha was not a girl to be scorned by anyone. "Oh... okay."

Great, now he'd hurt her feelings.

"You look amazing, and you know I'm down for it any other time. I've just been feeling lousy all day. I didn't even eat lunch." Not technically a lie.

Her countenance brightened.

"I'll get you some chicken noodle soup and nurse you back to health," she said silkily as she slid her finger down his chest.

"Samantha, stop acting like my girlfriend," he said firmly. "I'll text you when I'm feeling up to it."

"Okay, see you at school."

She quickly threw her jacket back on and headed for the door, but not before he saw tears welling up in her eyes. No doubt she'd cry all night, but he did not attempt to stop her. He would rather look at pictures of Juliette tonight than hook up with Samantha.

"Goodnight." She slammed his door shut, and he slumped to his bed, perplexed by his own actions. It was times like this that he missed his mom the most. A hug from her could ease some of the tension and anxiety that was plaguing his mind today. She could sometimes say only one word, but it was precisely the word what he needed to feel better. He swallowed hard against the acid in his throat and quickly put his sneakers on.

A run in the rain might help clear my mind, he thought as he walked past a thick haze in the living room.

"You alright, little bro? You've been in there all day." Mike was parked on the couch in front of the TV with his friend, Marty.

"Yeah, I'm fine... Just a lot on my mind." Ronan waved a cloud away from his face. "I told you not to do that in the house. Coach drug tests us all the time, and I can't afford to fail a drug test right now. You know I don't have a shot at a scholarship if I get kicked off the swim team," Ronan said tersely.

"Right, right. Sorry about that." Mike quickly shoved the joint in an ash tray on the coffee table. "Do you want to talk?"

What a joke, Ronan thought.

Mike wasn't someone he could confide in. After his parents died, Ronan used to call his grandfather whenever he was having a hard day. He never offered much advice, but he was a great listener. He would always respond with "sorry, son." It made Ronan feel like he still belonged to someone. When his grandfather died last year, Ronan had slipped into a dark depression. The best Mike could offer was a blunt and a beer.

"I don't feel like talking right now. I'm going for a run."

"It's raining!" Mike called after him.

He threw the door open, letting the cold rain pelt his face.

"Yeah. I know."

This weekend sucked.

Chapter 3

Juliette

JULIETTE SHIVERED AS SHE GOT OUT OF BED. It was unusually chilly for late April, even for upstate New York. She threw on her favorite thick green cardigan her grandmother had knit her years before. As she walked down the stairs, the knot in her stomach tightened with each step.

"Good morning, Jewels. Is something wrong?" This was probably the thirtieth time her mom had asked her since Friday. She had some kind of radar to recognize any change in Juliette's mood.

"No, I'm fine. You don't have to keep asking me. And don't call me Jewels. I thought Dad was coming home last night?"

Her dad was a truck driver and spent most of the week on the road. Juliette was a daddy's girl at heart.

"Nope. One more day," her mom sighed. "At least take this croissant with you. I put some peanut butter and honey on it."

"I'm not hungry."

Her mother's eyes widened, alarmed. "You need to start eating, young lady! You're skin and bones as it is."

"I feel a little stressed about my Calc test, that's all." A total lie.

"Eat this now. I won't let you leave until you do."

Juliette rolled her eyes. She ate the entire croissant in three bites and chugged her mom's coffee.

"Happy?" Juliette said with a mouthful of croissant.

Her mother shook her head. "Not really… but it'll do."

"I have to go. Lois is waiting for me." Juliette kissed her mother's cheek and hurried toward the door.

"Juliette!" Juliette turned around. Her mother's dark eyebrows were knit with concern.

"I hope you know that you can talk to me about anything. I'm on your side." Her mom gave her a sweet smile.

"I know, Mom." Juliette smiled back. *But if you knew I kissed Ronan Richland, you'd lock me in my room until graduation.* "Later gator."

Her mom grinned. "After a while, crocodile."

Juliette had one goal today; avoid Ronan as much as possible. It shouldn't be too difficult if she played her cards right. The only class they shared was Chemistry, and that was the last period of the day. They sat on opposite sides of the classroom, so there was little chance of interaction.

I'll be the last one in, and the first one out. Easy peezy lemon squeezy.

As she resolutely walked into school, the first person she saw was Ronan Richland. Her stomach dropped to her knees, and all her confidence evaporated.

Of course. Touché, Universe.

He was standing at his locker, looking like a dream. He was talking to Samantha Jones, which sent a trill up her spine.

Get a clue, Samantha. He's obviously bored to death with whatever you're saying.

His eyes met hers for the briefest of moments. She quickly looked straight ahead, refusing to meet his eyes again, and commanded her cheeks to keep their cool. She walked as quickly as she could without drawing attention to herself and took her seat in Calculus, pulling her textbook onto her desk. Suddenly, every problem became a jumble of numbers and letters that she couldn't decipher.

This is going to be long day.

Chapter 4

Ronan

RONAN HAD BARELY BEEN LISTENING to a word Samantha said. She was chatty for this early on a Monday. He watched the hall for Juliette like a hunter waiting for its prey. Every girl that looked even remotely like her sent his heart rate soaring.

"Can you believe she would say that? And after what happened this summer too!" Samantha babbled on incessantly.

"Uh huh," Ronan responded as he focused on the hall where he knew Juliette usually came from. Finally, she popped around the corner. She was looking down at her phone and tucking her long blonde hair behind her ear. She looked up and met his gaze for only a moment, then stared straight ahead and breezed past. Her expression was unreadable. He couldn't believe that she would be indifferent. He craned his neck as he watched her walk down the hall, hoping she'd turn around and give him some clues. He suddenly wondered if he had fantasized the entire thing.

"Ronan!" Samantha snapped.

He tried to replay the last ten seconds of what he'd heard, but his mind was blank.

"Yeah, I agree," he said lamely.

"I was trying to tell you a story about Beth and James. You didn't hear any of it?"

"Sammy, you know it's hard to follow when you talk so fast." He tried giving her a winning smile. Samantha's faced turned hot red, and her dark eyes blazed.

"Well, I guess you just don't have time for me today," she said.

She'll probably slash my tires if I don't fix this.

"You look really nice today!" He yelled as she stomped away. Samantha didn't so much as turn her head to acknowledge him, but Juliette whirled around to look at him. Their eyes met for a moment before she darted around the corner.

The entire day passed like a dream. Ronan had been hopeful school would distract him; snap him out of it. Being in the same building as Juliette intensified the restlessness that he usually felt on a normal school day. She would be in Chemistry class. Seeing her would make him feel better, and maybe give him an idea as to what his next move should be. He was usually the last one in, if he wasn't skipping. Today he was the first in his seat. Mr. Birch looked at him like he was insane, which was befitting; he was losing his mind. Students slowly filtered in, each one making Ronan's heart skip a beat.

Juliette was the last to walk in, and his heart did a full belly flop. He was completely distracted by how sinfully hot her butt looked in her skinny jeans as she walked past him. He could just imagine curling up on the couch under some blankets, wrapping his hands around her tiny waist, her hair cascading all around him... he had to stop himself from going any further. Mr. Birch gave Juliette a stern look and she gave him a quick "sorry" before taking her seat. Ronan did his best not to stare at her through the entire class. She didn't look in his direction once. He had never seen anyone so engrossed in Chemistry. After an agonizing 90 minutes, the bell rang. Juliette threw her books into her bookbag and hurried out the door, but he easily caught up to her. He was a runner and a swimmer, after all.

"Juliette!"

She was nearly sprinting at this point. Ronan had to jog to catch up.

"Jewels! You deaf?"

"I'm not deaf... and don't call me Jewels."

"Got it - sorry. Do you think we could talk?"

"There's nothing to talk about."

"Harsh. You don't remember that sexy kiss you planted on me three days ago?"

Juliette slapped her hand over his mouth.

"What is wrong with you?" she hissed.

Her temper was having the unwanted effect of entertaining him, rather than deterring him.

"Okay, I'm sorry. Seriously though, can we talk? Let's go to Steam Stop and get some coffee. On me."

"*No.* I have a boyfriend. I can't just go to a coffee shop with another guy."

"I think you're forgetting that *you're* the one that kissed *me*. Just say you're tutoring me for Chemistry, if you're really worried about getting in trouble."

She glared at him.

"I am doing pretty terrible in Chem. You can tutor me and in exchange I'll keep quiet about us."

Juliette sighed. She shifted her weight. "I dunno."

"Don't make me resort to blackmail," he teased.

"Like what?" She asked, biting the side of her lip.

He leaned forward and whispered, "I could invite Todd out for a coffee instead. We'd have a lot to talk about."

Juliette groaned loudly. "Okay, fine! Let me tell Lois I don't need a ride home..."

"Great! I'm parked in the south lot. I'll pick you up by the door. See you in a few minutes."

Ronan rushed to get to his car before she could change her mind. He had to clear out about a week's worth of trash in the passenger's seat. This felt like a victory for reasons he couldn't pinpoint, but right now he didn't feel like sorting that out. He just wanted a few minutes to talk to this girl who ruined sleep for him all weekend.

Chapter 5
Juliette

JULIETTE COULDN'T HELP BUT WONDER how many girls had sat in this exact seat. A nagging voice told her she shouldn't be doing this, but she tucked it away. They kept the conversation light in the car; she wanted to keep her distance. She sat on her hands awkwardly, not wanting to even touch his things.

Getting too familiar with Ronan would be like trying to pet a cheetah because it looked cute. She was liable to get her heart torn out, the way Robin, a junior in her youth group, had earlier that year. Ronan had shown her a lot of attention, and Robin had mistakenly thought they were an item. When Ronan made it clear that they were friends with benefits and nothing more, Robin was devastated. Juliette had spent a whole evening soothing Robin and giving her pep-talks about self-worth. "Guys like Ronan will never see how special you are," she remembered telling Robin at the time.

And look at me now. Sitting in Ronan's car, like the world's biggest hypocrite. How did I get myself into this situation?

Juliette was grateful Ronan picked a coffee shop on the outskirts of town. People in this town had known her since birth; if anyone from church saw her, they would surely call her mother. She grabbed her Chemistry book, guarding her heart with it. Ronan looked at her curiously.

"This probably comes as a shocker, but I don't really want to study," Ronan smiled, his divine dimples threatening her heart rate.

"Well then why did you bring me here?"

He didn't answer. Just kept a soft smile and looked at the ground.

"After you, M'lady," Ronan butchered an English accent as he held the door open for her.

Juliette couldn't hide a smile. *Cute but sad attempt at being charming.*

At the counter she ordered a small white chocolate latte, wrapping her hands around the mug, trying to soak in some of its warmth. Ronan ordered a large coffee with cream and sugar.

Not much for fluff, I guess.

When he got his coffee they picked a little booth in the back.

"So, Ronan, why am I here?" she held her head high and looked him directly in the eyes. She wanted to appear confident, even if her knees were knocking under the table.

"Well, '*Juliette*,' I've spent all weekend thinking about you. What was that kiss all about?"

"It was a dare. I don't see what the big deal is," she said, feigning confidence.

"It was more than a dare. Don't give me that." Ronan narrowed his eyes, crossed his arms, and leaned in toward her. "I know you felt something too."

Juliette couldn't think of a response. Her cheeks blazed as he leaned in closer.

"Do you have a crush on me or something?"

Juliette nearly choked. "How *dare* you. How full of yourself are you? I do *not* have a crush on you. I don't want to talk about his anymore." She crossed her arms and looked away, irritated.

"Why not? It was a great kiss, Juliette. If one little kiss was that hot, imagine what else we could do."

Juliette stood and considered coming across the table to smack him unconscious. "This is what's going to happen: you will forget about it, and so will I. I was stupid and impulsive. I shouldn't have done it." She could feel hot tears threatening to ruin her moxie. "I'm sick of people like *you* thinking I'm some boring prude. I'm just as good as any girl *you've* been with, and I wanted you to know that. Now it's over, and I don't want to think about it ever again."

She huffed and sat back in the booth. She didn't know what came over her. Her tongue had moved faster than her brain.

Now Ronan was dumbfounded. They stared at each other for a few seconds. Her heart was beating so hard, she worried he would hear it.

"I'm sorry I made you feel that way. I'm a jackass, I know it. I was just joking around with you. Teasing you. Sometimes guys tease cute girls, you know," he said.

How can he compliment me with such a straight face? She hated that she was already softening to him. There was no way to prevent her blushing, as much as she tried. *Stupid pale skin.*

Ronan cleared his throat. "I won't say anything else about it, I swear. I'm sorry I upset you. Let's talk about something else. What are you planning on doing after graduation?"

Juliette took a deep breath, relieved at the subject change. "I plan to take classes at Oswego Community College and become a math teacher. I'm good at math, and it's a steady job. I can probably find a job around here." It sounded so bland as it came out of her mouth.

Ronan nodded. "Then marry Todd, have 2.5 kids, and get a dog?"

She could have taken offense at this, but she studied his face and decided it wasn't an insult. She sighed and swirled the coffee in her mug. "I don't know. Honestly, I've been feeling so restless lately. Maybe I *am* playing it too safe. Maybe I'm supposed to do more. I just worry I'll be a disappointment if I end up making a mistake."

"Who are you worried about disappointing?"

"My parents, Todd, people at church, God. People expect me to be perfect. It's hard to keep that up."

31

She hadn't spoken to anyone about how unsettled she felt, couldn't even admit it to herself or God, and here she was telling Ronan Richland about it over coffee.

"Maybe you need to take a risk, Monte. Go and have an adventure," Ronan smiled kindly.

"Ha! Me having an adventure. Wouldn't that be something."

She crossed her arms, suddenly feeling vulnerable. "What about you, 'Richland'? Any big plans?"

"Yeah, to get the hell out of this shi-" he looked up at her and caught himself. "Get out of Avalon. As soon as possible."

She bit her lip to avoid smiling. *Super cute that he doesn't want to cuss in front of me.* "Why is that?" She asked.

Ronan stared at his coffee. He didn't speak for a few moments, so she waited.

"There's nothing here for me," he said quietly. "After Mom and Dad died, this cloud came over me. I can't get rid of it here, maybe I can run away from it."

He glanced up at her and studied her face. She wondered what he saw. Eventually he continued, "I've done really well on the swim team this year. I'm hoping I can get a good scholarship from that. My parents left me and my brother a lot of money when they died in that accident, but I'm pretty sure he's blown through most of it. I don't want to ask him for money either. I don't want anything from him."

Juliette could hear heavy bitterness in his voice. She remembered his parents had died suddenly in a car accident when they were in 5th grade. She didn't see much of Ronan or Mike after that, as they abruptly stopped going to church. Mike was known at school as the go-to guy for weed, or any other party supplies, but she didn't know much about him other than that.

"Mike is a waste of space. I have to get away from him. I hate him sometimes," his voice quavered and his knuckles turned white as he gripped his mug tighter. "Jesus. Can we change the subject? Tell me a joke or something."

Juliette had to plant her feet to keep herself from jumping to his side of the booth to hug him.

"Okay," Juliette replied. She cleared her throat. "Yo' momma is so fat she doesn't need the internet. She's already worldwide."

Ronan shook his head, loosening the grip on his mug. "Aw come on. You can do better than that."

"Yo' momma is so dumb, when I told her it was chilly outside, she brought a spoon." Juliette smiled as Ronan started chuckling. Not wanting to lose momentum, she blurt out another, "Yo' momma is so fat, when she got on the scale it said, 'I need your weight not your phone number.'" That sent him roaring. She continued to relay the very best of her extensive 'yo' momma' jokes, just to keep him laughing. Every time he did, his dimples showed.

No wonder he has girls falling at his feet.

They continued talking and joking effortlessly. Time seemed fluid, until Juliette noticed the sun setting outside.

"Good grief, it's 6 pm!" She tapped her watch, to see if it was working. It was.

"Who says 'good grief?' And who uses a watch? You're adorable."

A kaleidoscope of butterflies burst in her chest, she tried hard to ignore it. "I think you better take me home. My parents will be wondering where I am."

"Must be nice," he muttered under his breath. "Alright, let's go."

She hurriedly put her coat on and walked toward the door.

There was no lull in conversation on the way home. None of the awkward silences that she often experienced with Todd. Ronan's teasing was light and friendly. Maybe he had gained a little more respect for her after all. She was genuinely disappointed when he pulled up her driveway.

"Thanks for the coffee. And the company." She gave him a tender smile.

"Any time, Princess."

She got out, then quickly turned around and handed him her chemistry notes.

"Don't you need these?" he asked.

"I think you need them more. I didn't see you write a thing down in class today. Don't fail chemistry, Ronan. You're too smart for that. See you around."

Juliette floated to her front door. Things wouldn't be awkward now, Ronan was just a regular, cool guy after all.

A completely normal, gorgeous, dreamy guy.

Chapter 6

Ronan

RONAN PULLED IN HIS DRIVEWAY and turned the ignition off. He realized his cheeks hurt from smiling so much. Juliette was so easy-going. He didn't have any of the normal underlying dread he usually carried with him, and it was such a relief. He didn't feel like he needed to put up any front with her. She was a genuine person, not to mention delectable and funny. Her wacky sense of humor reminded him of his dad; he remembered his dad telling him some of those exact same 'yo' momma' jokes. Except back then he would groan and roll his eyes. Who knew he would miss all his dad's jokes this much one day? He put his seat back and stared at the roof of his car. Walking into his smoke-filled house to look at his drunk brother wasting his life away on the couch would immediately change his mood, so he usually waited until the last second before walking through the door.

He looked through his phone and thought about following Juliette on Instagram, but then she'd probably start looking through his stuff, and that was a bad idea altogether. There were one too many wild party pictures that she didn't need to see. Last year hadn't been a stellar year for him. After months of missing school and swim practices, his coach suspended him. He had to beg on his knees and promise with his life that he would make more of an effort this year. Getting a scholarship was his only hope of getting out of this God-forsaken town. His worst fear was turning into his brother. His second greatest fear was living with him for another year. He was a solid swimmer who had won his team several medals, otherwise his coach would not have given him a second chance. He had done everything he could to make his senior year better, other than the occasional girl here and there. Now he had a reason to think twice about that too.

He stopped on the picture of her at homecoming. He zoomed in to look at her eyes, her lips, her neckline.

How did I get in this weird situation? This wasn't supposed to happen.

His only plan was to get out of here. Get out of this town.

Stay focused Ronan. You don't have time for girls.

He huffed and dropped his phone in his lap, and picked up the papers she had given him. She was a pretty diligent note-taker. Why anyone would care so much about high school chemistry was beyond him. He had heard that smart people had bad handwriting, but hers was next level; he could barely make out the words.

Makes sense, she's such a cute little nerd.

There was a little doodle in the corner. After squinting for a few moments, he could make out a little pig. He smiled to himself, tore the pig off, and stuffed it in his pocket.

He thought back to his conversation with Juliette. If he was honest with himself, he'd never talked to a girl like that. Or anyone, for that matter. Even with his reputation as a "player," he'd never had what he would consider a "girlfriend." Indeed, many girls had tried to lock him down, but he had no interest. After his parents died, he hadn't opened up to anyone and hadn't wanted to, until now. It was a warm, somewhat frightening sensation. And

Juliette, of all people! Could they even really be friends? She had a family, a best friend, and hell she even had a boyfriend. She didn't need him, and probably didn't have the time or energy for him; and yet she'd spent almost three hours with him today.

He tried imagining a conversation like that with someone like Samantha. It would be impossible. Ninety percent of what spewed out of her mouth was either gossip or dirty talk. What had she even been talking about this morning? Whatever it was, it was painful to listen to. He pinched the bridge of his nose and squeezed his eyes shut. All of this thinking was giving him a headache, not to mention the lack of sleep, and that coffee. He hadn't had caffeine in four weeks.

Maybe Juliette is the bad influence after all. He grinned at the absurdity of the thought.

He took one final deep breath made his way inside. Mike was usually passed out by 7 pm, so he could avoid a confrontation with him. He sometimes felt guilty ignoring Mike as much as he did, but his brother had become an emotional drain. Mike looked so much like his mother; it was like a cruel joke. He walked past the clock in the kitchen and realized he had wasted almost two hours in the car, not entirely out of character for him.

Tomorrow is Tuesday. I have Chemistry on Tuesdays, he comforted himself in the thought.

He couldn't wait to see Juliette again. For the first time in ages, he was excited to go to school. What a weird week it was turning out to be.

Chapter 7
Juliette

JULIETTE TOOK A DEEP BREATH as she walked into her house. She needed to get her head straight before she faced her mother.

Her four-year-old brother Markus zipped past her, half naked, hollering, "No! No! No!"

"Hey, honey! I'll get dinner together as soon as I catch this little booger and get him bathed," her mother said as she walked by.

Thank God she's preoccupied.

"Lois is waiting for you in your room, by the way!"

"Okay, thanks."

She slowly walked up the stairs to her room. What was Lois doing here? When she told Lois she was leaving to tutor Ronan Richland, Lois had grabbed her and demanded more information. She had to pry herself away, promising to explain later. She had completely forgotten to come up with a reason, now she had to scramble for an excuse. She paused before she turned the knob and plastered on a smile.

"Hi, Lois!"

Lois was sitting on her bed with her arms and legs crossed, a hard glare in her eyes. Juliette got the sense that she was in big trouble.

"Hi yourself. Would you mind telling me what you and Ronan were 'studying' the last *two hours*?"

Juliette plopped on the bed next to her. "Geez, what are you, my mom? Ronan is failing Chemistry, so I'm helping him. That's all..."

Lois grabbed Juliette's face, forcing her to make eye contact. "You are such a terrible liar."

Juliette groaned and buried her face in her pillow. She couldn't keep this front up, not with Lois. "Listen. I have to tell you something, but promise you won't freak out! And you can't tell *anyone*."

Lois glared at her. "Okay?"

Juliette took another deep breath. "I kissed him."

Lois's jaw dropped. There were a few moments of silence followed by an explosive, "WHAT!"

Tears filled Juliette's eyes. "I know this sounds bad. Just let me explain!"

"You're serious? Have you lost your mind? We are talking about Ronan Richland, and not Todd Parker, your *boyfriend*?"

"Yes, but listen! Please!"

Lois gaped at her, incredulous. "Oh, I'm all ears."

Juliette did her best to explain. Lois's eyes were as big as teacup saucers.

"I must be hallucinating. So, are you guys together now?"

"No! *No*. It was just a stupid little thing. It's over now."

"Sure, okay." Lois leaned in with her head in her hands, and her expression changed from horrified shock to giddy curiosity. "So, what was it like?"

"What do you mean?"

"Tell me all about it. I want *details*."

Juliette paused, then she smiled. "It was... nice."

They both burst out laughing. "I'm serious! It was awesome. But it was a one-time thing, and only because he dared me."

"Why? I think you should go for it. You and Todd are old news now. He needs someone to light a fire under his butt, and so do you." Lois was constantly trying to push Juliette out of her comfort zone. When she and Todd had first started dating, she teased Juliette for being a "goody-two-shoes." Lately she had just been pushing for them to end it. She called them "the world's most boring couple."

"That's what's nice about our relationship though... there's no pressure."

"I think you mean 'no pleasure.' You need a little action. I'm on team Ronan. Oh my God! Ronan and Juliette!"

"Okay, you need to stop! There's nothing between us. We're just friends."

"Yeah we'll see. I wonder what Todd would do if he found out?"

"Honestly, he hasn't paid much attention to me lately. It might be nice to make him a little jealous. At least it would feel like he cared about me."

Lois closed her eyes shook her head dramatically. "Oh, sweet Juliette. Therein lies your problem."

"Girls! Come eat!" Juliette's mother called from the kitchen.

Later that night as Juliette lay in bed, her mind kept wandering between Ronan and Todd. It was exhausting. *Lord, I think I need help here. Get my mind right. Please!*

Chapter 8

Ronan

RONAN BOUNCED OUT OF BED ON TUESDAY. He blasted The Killers on the ride to school and sang as loud as he could. He strut down the senior hall like a king, until he caught sight of Todd talking to Juliette at her locker.

A tingle shot up his spine. Before he could analyze what that meant, he walked right up and threw his arms heavily around both their shoulders. Todd was considerably shorter than him which no doubt made Todd look foolish, precisely what Ronan intended. Ronan grinned impishly.

"Good morning, beautiful people!"

Todd was not amused. He adjusted his glasses. "I'm sorry, do you need help with something?"

In Middle School, Ronan had locked Todd in his locker more than once, and often stole his lunch. In his mind at the time, it was just 'joking around.' Those weren't his best years. He'd given up on that in recent years, but apparently, Todd could hold a grudge.

"Just giving Jewels her Chem notes back. They were super helpful. No wonder you always do so well." He playfully patted the top of her head.

Todd raised his eyebrows at Juliette. His eyes darkened as much as her face reddened.

"We're in the same class. Ronan is failing so I let him borrow my notes," she explained, sounding a bit desperate.

"Well, a low 'C' isn't failing. So what's new?"

Juliette gave Ronan a cautioning look. He merely grinned back.

"I'm trying to convince Juliette to do a solo at youth group Friday night if you must know."

"A solo? Do you sing, Jewels? Dang, that's awesome! Can I come?"

"It's at a church, Ronan," Todd hissed sarcastically.

"I used to go to your church. Are you saying I'm not welcome?" Ronan swallowed the desire to say more. He didn't want to look like a complete jackass to Juliette.

"Of course, you're welcome," Juliette quickly responded. Todd gaped at Juliette, incredulous.

"It starts at seven," she said.

"Great! I'll be there. See you in Chem, Princess."

Ronan knew that last word would sting Todd a little, and it made him smile to himself as he walked off.

I probably shouldn't have messed with him so much in Middle School, he thought, *but that tool deserved it.*

Chapter 9

Juliette

S TILL STANDING IN THE HALLWAY where Ronan left them, Juliette felt the heat of Todd's glare. "What exactly is going on here?"

"What do you mean?"

"Why are you suddenly all cozy with Ronan Richland?"

Juliette huffed. "Since when is inviting people to church considered 'cozy'? Aren't we supposed to be inviting people to church?"

"Sure, some people. Not him!"

"You can't be serious, Todd. If anyone needs Jesus, it's Ronan."

"Do you know how he treated me in seventh grade?" Juliette could see real hatred in Todd's eyes. This ugly side of the all-too-perfect Todd Parker was new, and it was seriously repulsing.

"I know he was a jerk, and he can still be, but we're supposed to be forgiving people, aren't we? That was almost five years ago. You aren't always nice to everyone either, and you know he's been through a lot. He lost both his parents when he was just a kid. He hasn't had a perfect life like *you*." He pursed his lips at her. "And me..." she added, realizing she was in the same judgmental boat most of the time.

Todd's dark eyes were blazing hot orbs now. "So, I guess this means you'll do the solo?"

"That's what it looks like," she answered, matching his sarcastic tone.

"Wonderful. Everything is just perfect now."

"Seriously, Todd, can't you just be happy that I said I'd do it? What is the problem?"

"I told you, everything is perfect; I'm perfect, you're perfect. We're all perfect. See you later, 'Princess.'" He spun on his heels and walked away.

Juliette stormed off down the hall. Lately, she couldn't seem to figure out why they had gotten together in the first place. Maybe she was just trying to appease her mother. She'd certainly never given him a thought before the day that he had asked her to be his girlfriend almost a year ago, but her mother had been so ecstatic that she felt pressured to say yes. What harm could it do? Their mothers had been best friends since High School. On the outside it seemed like they were a match made in heaven.

Ronan had been a jerk just then, but it was kind of nice to see someone stand up to Todd. Ronan and Todd were different in almost every way. Ronan was tall, dark, and muscular with penetrating blue eyes. He was jovial, outgoing, and charismatic. His smile could light up a room.

Todd was more like a burst of gloom. He was good-looking by most standards, with dark hair and dark brown eyes, but short and artsy rather than athletic. He had rock solid morals, which she admired about him. He had set clear physical boundaries in their relationship on day one and was diligent about keeping them. He was more interested in their "spiritual" relationship.

46

His intellectual mind could point out things in reading the Bible that she would never have noticed. She was in awe whenever he shared those thoughts with her, but in casual settings he seemed so uptight. Ronan was such a breath of fresh air to be around. Still, though, Ronan needed to keep his mouth shut. He was becoming a real problem, and now he was coming to hear her sing! She groaned loudly. Everyone in the hallway around her stopped to stare.

"I'm fine! I'm fine. Nothing to see here." She laughed awkwardly and ducked into her next class. Maybe she would talk to Ronan after school, and ask him to cool it.

Chapter 10

Ronan

RONAN SMILED as Juliette walked up to him after chemistry.
"I would love to go for another coffee, but I've got swim practice in a half-hour. Can I take a rain check?"

Juliette rolled her eyes. "Why are you starting trouble with Todd?"

"What? I wasn't trying to be an ass. I was just joking around."

"Please don't start stuff. I know you like to stir up trouble."

"Honestly, I wasn't. So, do you not want me to go to church with you on Friday?"

"No, you should come! I think you'd like it. Our youth pastor is awesome." She reached out her hand. "Give me your phone and I'll put my number in."

Geez, this girl is confusing. What is her endgame? Ronan thought as he handed her his phone.

"I'll text you the details," she said after plugging in her number. She handed the phone back, her hand gently brushing his, sending electric shocks through his arm. "See you later!"

"Bye," he replied weakly. He looked down at his phone and noticed she had saved her number with a jewel emoji. He chuckled as he tucked it in his pocket.

Ronan sauntered to the pool building. His emotions and thoughts were in serious turmoil, a swim in the cold was exactly what he needed. It was the only time he could truly escape. After his parent's deaths, he would spend hours in his neighbor's pool. He would swim from one end to the other until they would politely ask him to go home. Today looked like it was going to be one of those days.

He was the first one there, as usual. Shortly after, Dre' Walker showed up. Ronan smiled at him, "You'll never beat me to that scholarship if you keep showing up late like this."

"I'm waitin' on you to give me some real competition. Last practice you were slower than a week in jail, " Dre' laughed, dropping his bags on the wet concrete next to the pool.

They had gotten pretty close over the last two years, to the dismay of Dre's mother. If Ronan wanted to get out of the house, and stay out of trouble, he'd call Dre'. Ronan's other friends only hung around because of what his brother was willing to offer them. Ronan knew they were using him, but having empty relationships seemed better than having none at all.

"Hey Dre', I need some girl advice," Ronan said as they put their caps on.

"Bro, you are asking the wrong dude. What makes you think I know anything about girls? You see me spending all my time here with you," Dre' laughed. He was a good-looking guy, tall and athletic, not to mention smart, funny, and quite the gentleman. No doubt he could get just about any girl he wanted.

"Still..."

Dre's mood shifted. "So, what's up?" Dre' asked. He was a preacher's son. Ronan knew he had high morals. He was always the sober guy at every party, and he stayed away from casual hook-ups. Ronan didn't understand why, but it somehow made him seem trustworthy.

"Do you know Juliette Monte?"

Dre' nodded.

"She kissed me on a dare on Friday, and things have been.... weird since."

Dre' seemed surprised. "Well, it's weird that Juliette would kiss you in the first place."

"Well yeah, but I mean I feel weird..." Ronan was not great at talking about his feelings. And honestly, he had no idea what was going on anyway.

"I mean it was a pretty heated kiss, you know? So, I tried to talk to her about it yesterday... took her to a coffee shop...and she refused to talk about it! But then she sat and talked to me about a bunch of other stuff for hours!"

"Mmhmm." Dre's forehead crinkled as he listened intently.

"And then this morning, she tells me to step back, but then turns around and asks me to come to church. Does this make any sense?"

"Sure does," Dre' said casually as he slipped into the water.

"Then what does it mean?" Ronan was aware that he sounded desperate, but he didn't feel as embarrassed around Dre' as he would others.

"She wants to be friends, man. Stop making it complicated."

Ronan slipped into the pool and thought over Dre's words. The cold water calmed his mind. He thought about being friends with Juliette. It seemed odd to be friends with a girl that hot and not be hooking up with her.

"Well, do you think Juliette and I could really be friends?"

"Yeah. Why not?"

"Well... I'm not exactly the type of guy that she'd normally hang around."

"I don't think it matters much. We were both in a Bible study on campus last year, and she's pretty cool. She could be friends with anyone. You, the janitor, my 90-year-old grandma. She doesn't put people in little boxes the way you do. I think you should go to that church... bust outta that comfort zone."

Dre' set up to push off the edge of the pool.

"You know, I've been asking you to come to my church for years. I'm hurt bro." He looked at Ronan and smiled, his teeth a brilliant white against his dark skin. "See you on the other side." And he took off.

"Cheater!" Ronan yelled, but he knew it didn't matter. He would crush Dre' regardless. The way that this swim year was going scholarships would soon be flying at him. He just had to hang on for a few more months.

Chapter 11

Juliette

RONAN HEEDED JULIETTE'S WARNING. They didn't talk at all the rest of the week, other than the occasional "hey" or "see ya" before and after class. Juliette told herself she was relieved, but a piece of her felt bitterly disappointed when he walked past her down the hall. She convinced herself on Friday that he really should go to church, so she worked the courage up to approach him after school. She had to jog to the parking lot to catch him before he left.

"Hey, Ronan!" She called out breathlessly.

Ronan turned, and a huge grin lit up his face. "Hey yourself."

Goodness, he's beautiful, and so cheerful. Keep your cool.

"You never texted me back."

Ronan cocked his head. "You think I should go tonight? I didn't want to piss you off, or start stuff with Todd."

"Yes, you should come!" *A little too eager, Juliette, reel it in.* "I'd be really happy if you came," she said, trying to sound more casual. "Todd can deal with it. We're just friends, right?"

Ronan smiled at her, but there seemed to be some sadness behind it. "Yeah Juliette, we're friends, but it would be weird going back to that church.

You know, after my parents got killed in that car crash, no one from that church came to check on me. No one."

This information rocked Juliette. She had never known anyone from New Life church to be anything less than self-sacrificing and helpful to everyone she knew. "Are you sure? What about my folks?"

"I'm telling you, no one checked on me. No phone calls, no visits, no meals, nothing. Crickets."

Juliette was dumbfounded. "There's got to be more to it than that…"

"Granted, Mike wouldn't take me anymore, but it would have been nice to hear from someone. Bring me some food or something. My parents had just died and all I ate was fast food for months."

Ronan took a deep breath and stared up at the sky. "Listen I know that doesn't have anything to do with you. Maybe I'll come for your sake. I'll think about it."

"Ok. I'll text you directions," she said tentatively. She scrambled her brain for some response to this revelation about her church, but she couldn't find a worthy one.

"This probably comes as a shocker, but I still remember where the church is. Later, Princess." With that, he opened the door to his BMW and drove off.

Juliette sighed. *Well, I did what I set out to do. The ball is in his court now.* Her phone pinged with a text from Lois.

I've been sitting in this car waiting for you for twenty minutes >:(

She took off before Lois gave up on her and left her stranded.

Chapter 12

Ronan

RONAN WAFFLED BACK AND FORTH on the way home. He drove into the empty parking lot of his old church and was hit hard with nostalgia.

Is this really a part of my life that I want to revisit?

Looking at the simple brick building brought back happy memories of going to church with his parents, having cookouts with the kids in his Sunday School class in the fall, and playing on the playground in the summer time. It also brought back the raw pain of losing his parents so suddenly, and the vacuum it created his heart.

He sighed heavily. *I should just go home and go to bed early.*

He had a big swim meet in the morning. In the last year, swimming had become the most important aspect of his life. It was the one place that he felt comfortable, and at times it seemed it was the only thing he was good at. This particular meet was against the best high school swim team in New York, and recruiters were expected to be there. He needed his mind in the right place to secure a good scholarship, get out of this town, and start a new life.

Then again, how big of a deal could a youth group meeting be? If he remembered correctly, it was a bunch of thirteen and fourteen-year-olds. Plus, he could hear Juliette sing, and see her in an environment other than school. He was annoyed by how intrigued he was by Juliette.

Maybe seeing her tonight will help me get over… whatever this is.

His stomach growled in protest. He looked at his phone. It was 6pm.

Enough time to grab a cheeseburger and talk myself out of this.

Whether he did or didn't go, he certainly wasn't going to let anything interfere with his chances of getting out of this dead-end town.

Chapter 13

Juliette

JULIETTE'S HEART BEAT LIKE AN ANGRY DRUM AGAINST HER CHEST. She decided to sing "Come Thou Fount" as her solo piece. It was rare to sing a hymn at youth group, but this one was special to her. It had been her grandmother's favorite song, and Juliette had sung it at her funeral a couple of years earlier. Even though she'd sung it a thousand times before, she was worried she'd forget all the words if Ronan Richland came strolling in. She was now re-braiding her hair for the fourth time. She was going to curl it around her head like a golden crown. Todd loved it that way, he said she looked like an angel. He was so select with his complements that when he did give one, she took note. Today, though, her hands kept shaking, and her braids kept coming out sloppy. She sighed, exasperated.

"I give up. Sloppy braid it is."

She was also having trouble deciding on what to wear. Nothing too flashy, homely, or desperate looking. She tried on three dresses and two skirts before she finally decided on skinny jeans, combat boots, a black turtleneck, and a jean jacket. It covered everything, and she still felt cute.

Perfect. You got this, Juliette.

She felt a little confidence boost as she slowly turned in the mirror. She stood up straight and took a deep breath in.

These nerves are stupid, she thought. *All this anxiety and he probably won't even show up.*

Then she'd feel like a real fool. Or would she feel like more of a fool if he did? She couldn't decide if she was dreading this night or looking forward to it. She put on some red lipstick, then wiped it off.

Too much.

Some of it has stained her lips, and she was trying to wipe it off when she heard Lois honking outside.

I really need my own car so I can come and go as I please, she thought, frustrated.

It was just as well. She needed to get her eyes away from this mirror. It was only stressing her out. She ran outside after kissing her mom on the cheek and opened Lois's car door.

"Well, hello, sexy!" Lois beamed at her. "Don't you look adorable?"

"What, seriously? Should I go change?"

"Um, why would you change, dummy? I just said you look adorable."

Juliette hurried in and shut the door.

"I dunno. I couldn't figure out what to wear tonight."

"For real? Why do you even care? Look at me!" Lois pointed to her sweat pants, then her sloppy top knot. "I don't even have any makeup on!"

Juliette smiled at her. "Lois, you barely ever wear makeup."

Lois laughed loudly. "True! Let's get this show on the road."

They were quite a pair, having almost nothing in common. Lois was crafty and outgoing. She thought the world was her own personal audience. Juliette was more of a studious and quiet bookworm. It worked, somehow. Lois had been Juliette's best friend since Lois found her alone on the playground in second grade and said, "We are best friends now." Juliette had just agreed then and never looked back. With Juliette's laid back and introverted personality, it was mostly a relief to have Lois take the lead in social situations. She imagined a life without Lois would be slightly dry.

Juliette quickly scanned the room when she walked in. No sign of Ronan. She spotted Todd waving at her frantically to come to the stage. He shut his guitar case hard and shook his head. She ran up to him, trying to figure out what he was mad at this time.

He finally looked up from the guitar he was tuning and said, "You're late."

"Todd it's only 6:45, how am I late?"

"I told you to be here at 6:45 at the absolute latest so that we could practice. Now we will be rushed. Grab a microphone. We're in a hurry."

His voice was overly irritated. It seemed a little overkill to be this upset over a youth group that rarely had more than forty kids in attendance. The 'performer' in him was something that she could not relate to.

You would think he's leading the symphony harmonic and not youth group worship at New Life Church in Avalon, New York. Juliette rolled her eyes. She grabbed the microphone and began singing along with his guitar. She kept an anxious eye on the door, but it was just the same old kids filtering in. They ran through the song twice.

"So, how was it?" Juliette asked.

"I could have used a little more practice, but it is what it is now," he said tersely. He looked up, took a deep breath and softened. "You were great, Juliette. You always are."

She curtsied. "Thanks! You sounded great too."

He rolled his eyes and smiled in response.

The sanctuary doors closed, and Pastor Vick stood up and opened the meeting with prayer. Juliette kept an eye on the door as inconspicuously as she could, but no sign of Ronan. By 7:15, all hope that he would show was gone, and she let out a breath that she didn't know she was holding. She had nothing to be nervous about now. As soon as Todd started playing, the back door opened, and Ronan sauntered in. Everyone turned to look, and he gave a sheepish grin as he settled in a rear seat. A roll of whispers traveled through the crowd, especially amongst the lower classman girls. Ronan smiled at her and nodded his head.

"I hope you guys will sing along with me," Juliette said shakily. "If you don't know the words, they'll be on the screen."

Juliette closed her eyes. *All right, Lord, I'm going to sing this to You. You and me, no one else in the room.*

Chapter 14

Ronan

R ONAN HAD TALKED HIMSELF IN AND OUT of going. He had fully decided on leaving as soon as he had arrived in the parking lot. He sat in the church parking lot for a good ten minutes before he got the courage to go in. How would it feel being in the church his parents took him to so many years ago? It wasn't that he'd avoided it. Mike had forbidden him from it as soon as his parents were in the ground. He had said, "No loving God would do this to us," and there had been no more discussion on the topic since then. At the time, Ronan had felt guilty, as if his parents would somehow be upset with him, but over time those feelings dissipated. Truthfully, he had not given it a thought since he had gotten his car, and Mike no longer had a say on where he went and what he did. After wrestling back and forth, and even turning the car on to leave, he groaned and got out.

Chill out, Ronan. It's just a church, nothing to worry about.

When he walked in, Juliette was on stage. As he slipped in his seat, she asked everyone to stand and sing along.

Fat chance.

He heard whispers from several groups of girls in front of him. One bold pre-teen even turned and winked at him. He immediately regretted walking in, but it was too late to slip out now. As soon she started singing, though, he was captivated. Not with her voice necessarily, it was nice, but with the conviction with which she was singing this song. She was putting her whole heart and soul in this, unabashed. He was spellbound.

When it was over, everyone was asked to sit down. It took Ronan a few seconds to recognize that he should also sit, but Juliette ran right to him and snapped him out of it. She looked delighted and incredibly pretty tonight.

"Can I sit here?" Her lovely brown eyes were having a powerful effect on him.

"Sure," he managed to choke out.

The pastor got up to speak, and everyone began quieting down.

Juliette leaned in. She smelled divine. "I'm so glad you came," she whispered in his ear, sending a tingle up through his spine.

"Thanks. You look gorgeous," he whispered back in her ear.

The moment evaporated as soon as Todd sat down next to her, with Lois close behind. Todd gave him a hard glare and took Juliette's hand. Ronan bit the inside of his lip until he tasted blood. A "Hey guys!" blared from the stage, drawing Ronan's attention, making him realize he was staring daggers at Todd's fingers laced with Juliette's.

Ronan shifted his gaze forward and focused on this "Pastor Vick." He was a young, good looking blonde in his early twenties. He was new; Ronan didn't recognize him from his childhood. The youth pastor then had been a dorky old guy who used puppets a little too much.

Why would anyone choose to come to this rinky-dink church in this rinky-dink town to talk to a bunch of teenage girls on a Friday night? Mind-boggling.

The "message" lasted about twenty minutes. Pastor Vick wasn't saying anything too profound, nothing new that Ronan hadn't heard from either church or his parents. The last bit of his message hit home, though.

"We've all got an expiration date on us, probably sooner than we think. Right now you guys all feel invincible, but none of us are. I want you all to be ready to hear these words when you face God, from Matthew 25:23 'Well done, good and faithful servant. You have been faithful with a few things; I will put you in charge of many things. Enter into the joy of your Lord.' Let's pray together, guys."

Ronan could feel a lump in his throat and hot tears in his eyes. His heart started racing as a flood of uncontrollable emotion was washing over him. He suddenly felt a suffocating panic as the realization hit that he was about to lose it, in front of Juliette Monte no less.

I have to get out of here.

He waited until everyone's heads bowed, especially Juliette's, and then he quietly slipped out the other end of the aisle. He managed to make it through the sanctuary doors, blinking hard. Before he could make it through the lobby and to the parking lot, he felt a small pair of hands wrap around his forearm.

"Ronan, wait!"

He took a deep breath, put on a smile, and turned around.

"Hey, are you okay?"

"Yeah! I have a big swim meet tomorrow. I need to get a full eight hours. You were great by the way."

He fumbled in his pocket, searching for his car key.

Get me the hell out of here.

Juliette's eyebrows knit together. "Okay, well I was going to see if you wanted to get some ice cream or something with us. We usually go out afterward."

"Is Todd going?"

"Well, yeah."

"Nope, I'm good. See you on Monday."

Before he could make it another step, Pastor Vick stepped next to Juliette.

"Hey there. Ronan, right?"

You have got to be kidding me.

"Yeah. Am I in trouble?"

"Trouble? That's hilarious. No trouble. I just wanted to introduce myself. I'm Pastor Vick."

"Oh. Hi." Ronan shook Pastor Vick's outstretched hand, wondering if he should say anything else.

Dude, please let me leave.

"I'm so glad you could come. I hope you decide to come back again sometime."

"Yeah, we'll see..."

Pastor Vick reached in his pocket. "I wanted to give you my card. It has my cell number on it. If you ever need anything, I mean anything, I'm available."

Ronan could tell by the earnest look in his eye that he was genuine.

Okay, weirdo.

"Alright, thanks. I gotta go."

"Sure thing! Nice to meet you, Ronan!"

"Yup, same."

And with that he took off, leaving Juliette and Pastor Vick behind. He didn't know what to think of that meeting. He did know one thing for sure. He was never going back.

Chapter 15

Juliette

JULIETTE TRIED SLEEPING IN ON SATURDAY, but her eyes popped open at 7 am. She lay in bed, mulling over the night before. Ronan had taken off so suddenly; something had upset him. Was it Todd's ridiculous behavior? But then Ronan didn't seem like the type to be easily intimidated. Was it something she had done? Maybe she was so excited that it was a turn-off? Or maybe it had something to do with the church itself. He did say that no one had checked on him after his parent's death, which she had a hard time believing. She thought about texting him, but it felt like crossing some boundary, since he had never texted her. She sighed. She might as well get up; this internal ping-pong game was getting her nowhere.

Juliette trudged downstairs. Her mom was sitting at the kitchen counter drinking coffee and doing her morning devotions; she was diligent about doing them early every day. Juliette admired that. She usually had to drag herself out of bed. She poured herself a cup of coffee, filled it generously with vanilla creamer and watched it swirl until her coffee was a light terra cotta brown. She pulled out a stool and sat next to her mom.

"Good morning. Am I bothering you?"

"Not at all, honey. I was just finishing up." She closed her notebook and Bible. "Do you think you could help me with some paperwork today?"

Her mom worked part-time as a paralegal and often brought work home for Juliette to help with. Juliette took care of any math; it was her specialty, and her mother's weakness.

"I already said I would." It came out snappier than she meant. That was happening more often lately, especially when she was tired. Her mother raised her eyebrows and gave her the "mom" look.

"Sorry," she muttered.

They sat in silence for a few moments.

"So, Mom... do you have any other plans today?"

Her mom shrugged. "About three loads of laundry and keeping a four and eighteen-year-old alive. Does that count?"

Juliette chuckled. "I guess. Is Dad coming home today?"

She and her mother were so similar in personality that they often butt heads. Her father broke up their fights; he was definitely the peacemaker of the family.

"No, tomorrow."

"Oh. Bummer." She felt more whole with her father in the house.

More silence. Finally, Juliette got to the real subject that was annoying her.

"Mom, do you remember a boy named Ronan Richland?"

Her mother's eyebrows raised. "Of course I do. It was one of the saddest things I had ever experienced when his parents passed away. Ronan looked so small and fragile at that funeral, it was horrific."

"So, what happened exactly? I've heard stories at school and all, but I never heard you talk about it before."

Her mother sat back and took a deep breath. "Well, they were very active members of our church, his mom and dad. They'd only gotten saved about three years before they passed. His dad was a physician in town, pretty well-known, and his mom was a kindergarten teacher. Such lovely people." Her mom teared up.

"They decided to go on a trip, I believe it was July. I think it was their twentieth anniversary, maybe? They were driving up to Bar Harbor, Maine. I remember her telling me that she was so excited but nervous about leaving Ronan with Mike for the first time. Mike was only nineteen and had just finished his first year of college, and Ronan had just turned ten. You went to his birthday party, do you remember?"

Juliette nodded.

"Well, anyway, they were only about two hours into the trip when wham! They were hit by a tractor trailer. Killed instantly. The truck driver had fallen asleep at the wheel."

"Then what happened?" Juliette's eyes were as big as saucers. She curled her toes around the bottom of the bar stool she was sitting on.

Her mother sighed. "Well, it turns out that his parents left everything in their will to Mike. The house, all the life insurance, and Ronan. I can't imagine

67

why they thought that was a good idea. From what I've heard through the grapevine, it was quite a chunk of money, around one million. I think the grandparents on his father's side offered to take Ronan, but they were quite elderly, and Mike refused to give him up. Mike ended up not going back to college, of course. We tried to stay involved as a church, but after the funeral, Mike wouldn't have anything to do with us. He actually slammed the door in Cathy Morgan's face when she tried to bring a casserole over. It was a shame, Ronan was a lovely little boy."

Juliette's jaw dropped open. "So that's it? You guys just gave up on them?"

Her mother frowned at her, "Honey, we tried. Pastor Drew tried calling and visiting. Your dad and I even offered to pick Ronan up for church. Mike refused. He had sole custody. There was nothing we could do."

"He was just a hurt little boy who had lost both his parents and then his church abandoned him too? How could you do that?" Tears were now streaming down her face.

Her mother put her hand gently on her shoulder. "Juliette, you need to calm down. Be reasonable."

Juliette shrugged her mother's hand away. "No! We talk about love all the time, but when one of our own needed us, we just gave up on them like they meant nothing."

She slammed her mug on the counter and ran to her room, locking the door behind her. She felt heartbroken for the little boy who must have suddenly felt utterly alone in the world. Juliette wanted to pull that little boy up in her arms and protect him from this cruel world. What would she be like now if she had experienced the same thing?

And I've judged him so many times. She felt the guilt creep into her heart. *Why didn't I reach out to him when it happened? We were in the same class.*

She remembered seeing him at school afterward, looking very somber. She was too shy to say anything to him.

I could have at least said "sorry."

She clearly remembered his party now. He had said, "I only invited you 'cause Mom made me. Girls are stupid." She had run into the bathroom, crying. Juliette laughed to herself at the memory. Ronan was just a normal kid then. He didn't deserve this. God's plans were so hard to understand sometimes.

She heard her little brother Markus run down the stairs screeching that he was starving. Juliette sighed and got up. Her mom needed her help, and she needed to get her emotions in check. She was becoming more and more impetuous every day.

She sighed and unlocked her door. *I need to apologize. Mom didn't deserve all that.*

Chapter 16

Ronan

RONAN HAD BEEN WORRIED that his emotional and restless night would interfere with his performance at the swim meet. He was so wound up, however, that he actually swam better than he ever had before. Several recruiters approached him afterward and asked about his college plans. By the end of the meet, he was soaring. As the crowds dispersed and he walked across the parking lot to his car, his elation dissipated and was replaced with a familiar toxic smog.

He stood at his car, watching Dre' walk out with his extensive family. For everything Ronan lacked in family, Dre' seemed to have it in abundance. He had asked Dre' to hang out afterward, but of course there was some big family function. He had invited Ronan, but the glare from Dre's mother told him that he wasn't really welcome.

It wouldn't have killed Mike to come to one competition.

Ronan had brought it up several times and reminded him as he walked out the door that morning. Mike had said, "yep, sure," and groaned and rolled over.

Ronan got in his car and contemplated which fast food joint he should hit up for lunch. He settled on a Big Mac, usually his favorite as far as fast food burgers go, but today it settled in his stomach like an angry brick. A year ago he would have called up any number of classmates, but these guys would only get him in trouble. He couldn't afford that.

I just need to hang on a few more months. Just get out of this town. He drove around aimlessly, trying to fill the empty space.

His mind kept returning to the evening before. He didn't know why Pastor Vick's words had hit him so hard. He'd teared up! He hadn't cried in years.

The last time he had cried was when he was eleven years old. He had gotten into a fistfight with Ronald Baker at soccer practice, which left them both with black eyes. Ronan had been kicked off the team as a result, since he had started it, and it was not his first offense. His coach had dropped him off when Mike did not show to pick him up afterward. Those were the days when Mike would disappear for days at a time, with no word on where he was. Ronan never told anyone; he was too terrified that he would become a foster kid, a threat that Mike regularly told him when he disappeared with his friends. Ronan had quickly learned how to take care of himself.

Ronan walked into his dark, empty house that day, past the pictures of his broken family, past his room and into his parent's bedroom, which was exactly as his mother had left it. He had laid on their bed and sobbed into their sheets for hours. No one came to comfort him, and the realization hit that no one ever would. He hadn't cried since.

Chapter 17

Juliette

THINGS WERE AWKWARD the following week at school. To Juliette, it seemed like Ronan was avoiding her, and she wasn't quite sure what she should do about it. Initially, she had seen him as a problem that she wanted to go away, but now that he had 'gone away' she was bothered more than ever. Why couldn't she stop thinking about him? She had prayed about it but wasn't getting much clarity. Doing the right thing wasn't always so simple.

At the end of the day on Thursday, Juliette walked to the parking lot to head home, but couldn't find Lois's car in their usual spot. Maybe they had parked in the East lot that morning? By the time she walked over, nearly everyone had left. No sign of Lois.

She dug her phone out of her book bag to call Lois and saw a text from her from two hours earlier.

Going home – puking my guts out! Call you later.

"Oh, crap..." she whispered.

Her phone was now at 10%. She quickly dialed her mom's cell. No answer. Her dad had left the night before, so no use calling him. She dialed Todd; nothing. She called her mom again; nothing. Now she was getting frustrated. She could be getting murdered out here, and no one would know. She walked toward the school, but the door was locked.

You have got to be kidding me.

What were they going to do anyway? Get her an Uber? She looked at the gray sky. It would only take her about an hour to walk home, but she might get stuck in the rain. She thought about calling her aunt, who lived 45 minutes away. Maybe she'd try Todd again first. As soon as she pressed send her phone died.

"Oh come on!"

"Hey, Princess." Ronan's voice came right behind her.

She nearly jumped out of her skin. She turned and punched him in the arm. "Don't sneak up like that!"

He laughed and rubbed his arm. "You got a nice hook there. I'm impressed." He was way too happy about this. She was not in the mood.

"Do you need a ride? Or are you staying here all night? I mean, I know you're a nerd, but that's a bit extreme."

She huffed. Maybe this was God's answer to her questions. Some sense of humor He had.

"Yes, I need a ride, but I don't want to put you out. Lois left early, and neither mom nor Todd will answer. I don't even know why they have phones." She rolled her eyes.

"Well, come on. I haven't talked to you all week. Plus, it's on my way home."

Juliette smiled. "It's the opposite of your way home, Ronan."

Ronan turned. "Whatever. Just come on."

She reluctantly got in his car.

After a few minutes, she finally spoke. She wasn't one for awkward silences. She liked to address the elephant in the room directly.

"Ronan, I'm sorry if that meeting was weird."

He looked at her. "What do you mean?"

"Just, if you felt uncomfortable, I'm sorry about that. I didn't mean for that to happen."

Ronan looked at her, incredulous. "If I felt uncomfortable, it's my fault. You shouldn't apologize for anything. You were great."

"Don't be silly. I'm an adequate singer if anything."

"You're way more than adequate Juliette, in every way."

He said it so casually and matter-of-fact that it caught her off guard, and she could feel her cheeks get hot. She wondered if every girl felt this way with him. They rode in silence for a few more minutes.

"It was just weird being back in church," he finally said. "I haven't given God much thought for the last few years. Obviously." He smiled at her sheepishly. "I guess after what happened to my parents, I just figured He didn't care too much about me."

"He does care about you, though. You know that, right?"

"No." Ronan huffed. "Why would I know that? How could that have happened if He cared so much?"

Juliette was silent. She had no answer.

"I don't know why things like that happen, Ronan. It doesn't make sense to me either. The only thing I *can* tell you with certainty is that He cares about you, and He didn't forget about you." She looked at him, concerned.

He smiled. "Yeah okay, okay. I know you think that. You don't have to look at me like that."

"Like what?"

"Like you're so concerned I'm on my way to hell."

Her jaw dropped.

"Don't lie, Jewels. You were thinking about it. I can read your face like a book."

When they pulled in, her mom was taking groceries in the house with her wild little brother, Markus, right behind her.

Her mother slowly looked at Ronan, then Juliette, then back to Ronan.

"Well, Lois sure has changed since this morning," she said.

"Lois got sick at school. I tried calling you." Juliette crossed her arms. "Of course you didn't answer."

"I was probably driving, Jewels." Her mother answered, mimicking her tone. She was no match for her mother. "Hi. I'm Juliette's mom, Mary."

Ronan extended his hand. "Pleased to meet you. I'm Ronan. Juliette and I are friends."

Her mother's eyebrows raised. "Ronan Richland?"

"Yes, ma'am. Let me get those groceries in for you!"

Before she could answer, he was in her car, grabbing a load.

"Well, okay, but then you'll have to stay for dinner. I'm sure you could use a home-cooked meal."

Juliette glared at her mom, away from Ronan's view. Her mother ignored her entirely.

Ronan beamed. "I'd love that. I haven't had one in years!"

He joyfully brought in all the groceries and then sat on the living room floor as her brother unloaded his dinosaur collection. Juliette joined her mother in getting dinner ready and kept an eye on them from the kitchen. Her mother kept giving her curious side eyes, which Juliette returned with hard "be cool" glares.

"Is there something going on here that I should be aware of?" Her mother whispered.

"Absolutely nothing, other than him giving me a ride home because I was stranded. You shouldn't have invited him to stay," Juliette hissed back.

"Well, you are the one who guilted me the other day. Are you changing your tune now?"

"You're a few years late now, aren't you?"

Her mother looked hurt.

"Okay, sorry, you're right. It's just that he has a reputation that I don't want sticking to me in any way..."

"People always talk, Juliette. You can't live your life by what people say about you. He seems like a nice boy to me, and I'm an excellent judge of character."

Juliette sighed and set the table. Ronan had Markus pinned to the floor and was tickling him, making him laugh hysterically. Todd wouldn't be caught dead doing anything so undignified.

Maybe she's right. He's not so bad.

Once they sat to dinner, it was as if Ronan were a regular guest. He was just as charming to her mom as he was to anyone else. The perfect gentleman. Juliette watched him carefully, wondering if this was an act, or if this was the real Ronan. By the end of the night, her mother had stars in her eyes.

"Before you leave, Ronan, let me pack you up some leftovers."

"I would love that, Mrs. Monte. Dinner was incredible, way better than fast food," he laughed.

If this is an act, he deserves an Academy Award, Juliette thought as she walked him to his car.

"Thanks for the ride, Ronan, and for helping my mom and playing with my brother. I owe you."

"Well, then how about a kiss on the cheek?"

Juliette stood aghast. "Wh... what?"

"Relax, Jewels, I'm joking. See you tomorrow."

"Oh, okay. See ya."

He shut the door and drove off.

It took Juliette awhile to realize that she was standing in the yard, staring after his car, frozen in time. When she turned to walk in, her mother was standing on the front steps with her eyebrows raised and a knowing smile on her face.

"Now I understand why you were so curious about Ronan Richland."

"He's a friend," Juliette said firmly.

Her mom looked at her skeptically. "Okay. Come on in and help me clean up."

Juliette walked in dreamily. She didn't need to explain herself.

Chapter 18

Ronan

RONAN HUMMED HAPPILY the following day after school. He'd just met with the school counselor to go over his options from the many colleges that were trying to recruit him. He was 99% settled on the University of Texas. It seemed far away, exotic even. The fact that it was far away was the only criteria that he was looking for; that and the fact that they were offering a full scholarship sealed it. Freedom was so close. They offered the same scholarship to Dre' and they had talked about it at swim practice. His dreams were becoming a reality; it was so sweet he could taste it. And he couldn't wait to taste the leftover lasagna that Juliette's mom had given him, so he was bitterly disappointed to find it gone when he opened the fridge.

"Mike! Did you eat my leftovers?"

"Yeah, they were awesome. Where did you get that?"

"It was from a friend. Don't eat my stuff." He slammed the refrigerator door shut.

"Why're you home so late, little bro?" His brother lumbered in the kitchen.

"I was at swim practice. What else."

"Oh right. When is that big meet again?"

Ronan rolled his eyes. "It was Saturday."

"Oh damn. Sorry. How did you do?"

He couldn't stand being in the same room as his brother these days. As a kid, Ronan had looked up to him. Now he could barely look at him at all. Overweight, disheveled, smelling like an old beer bottle.

"Why even ask, Mike?" With each passing day the end of this living arrangement became more of a reality, and he cared less and less about sparing his brother's feelings.

"What is that supposed to mean?" Mike's voice had a bite. He had quite a temper, but he was no longer able to tower over Ronan and so it didn't have the same effect it used to.

"You obviously don't care so don't pretend. It doesn't matter to me anymore."

"Don't care? Don't care?" His voice kept getting louder with each word. "I gave up everything for you. Why don't you show some respect," he snarled, pressing his finger deep into Ronan's chest, "and quit acting like a whiny brat all the time. I'm sick of your preteen girl emotions."

"Gave up everything? What a load. You haven't been there for me once."

Mike's eyes were boiling now. He took a slow step closer toward Ronan, and Ronan instinctively stepped back.

"Every dream I ever had died with mom and dad. I had to become a parent and an orphan in one day. I fed you, washed your dirty underwear, and cleaned your damn vomit up when you puked. I even bought you that stupid car for your 16th. Do you have any idea how much that cost?" His voice was low and steady, which was somehow more frightening than his yelling.

Ronan pursed his lips, wondering if he should back down. *No. I always back down.* "That wasn't your money, Mike."

Mike's heavy hand swiped across Ronan's face before he could react. Ronan clenched his jaw and pressed his eyes shut. A hot drip of blood slipped through his lips, filling his mouth with a sickening metallic taste. He took a deep breath, trying to force the rage out of his chest. *It's not worth it.* He grabbed his keys off the counter.

"Don't wait up," he said as he pushed past Mike's shoulder.

Chapter 19

Juliette

JULIETTE SPENT SATURDAY MORNING and afternoon helping Lois at a craft show. Lois made little knick-knacks like jewelry and hair bows and sold them to whomever she could. Lois gave Juliette 20% for hanging out with her for the day, which amounted to a whole $12. Juliette sighed when she got in the car. It wasn't even worth the gas money to get there. She needed to get a side job.

When she got home, her mom was finishing up her favorite casserole, chicken enchiladas.

"Awesome." Juliette smiled.

"Good! You're home. I want you to take this to Ronan Richland."

"Um, excuse me? No way."

Her mother looked at her sideways. "Weren't you the one lecturing me about helping him out?"

"Mom, I was saying you should have helped him back then, not now! I don't want to go there. It would be weird."

"He didn't seem weird at all when he was here. He was lovely, actually. You said we should be helping people. You can't have it both ways. Take it over." She pushed the dish into Juliette's hands.

Juliette groaned. "Mom! Please, no!"

Her mother gave her a stern look. She knew there was no way out. "I've written the directions to heat it right on top. Take it over now in case they want it for dinner. It's already 5."

Juliette reluctantly took the dish and walked to the car. Knocking on his door would be humiliating, and yet it would give her a chance to see his home. She was pretty curious about how he lived. She couldn't imagine having been raised by a 19-year-old brother. She also wanted to meet Mike, the man who had sacrificed so much for his little brother. She wondered if he had Ronan's good looks. His dark hair, his dreamy blue eyes, and his offset, adorable dimples. The thought was so consuming that she drove right past his house and had to turn around.

Her heart stopped momentarily as she rang the doorbell. She prayed hard that no one was home, although Ronan's car was in the driveway. Ronan answered seconds later with a bewildered look on his face. "Juliette?"

"That's me! I have a gift for you. From my mother." She held forth the casserole.

Ronan took it and then looked at her, confused. "Why would she do that? And why is it cold?"

"I guess you made some impression on her, you charmer! And you have to cook it, silly." She pointed to the top. "The directions are right here."

"Well, I don't know what to do with that."

She stared at him to see if he was serious. He was.

"Ronan you just pre-heat to 325 and pop it in for 45 minutes."

"Well, I can't do that. No one has turned that oven on in eight years. I doubt it still works, and even if it does, I don't know how to use it."

Juliette gave an exasperated sigh. "Are you for real? Who doesn't know how to turn on an oven?"

He shrugged.

She took the casserole from him and pushed past him into the foyer. The house was dark and dusty, but not overly filthy as she had expected.

"Where is your kitchen?"

He pointed straight back and then followed her like a puppy.

The kitchen certainly didn't look like it got much use. Juliette set the casserole on the counter and opened the oven.

"Well, it looks clean."

"I just told you, the thing hasn't been used it in eight years. It ought to be clean."

She quickly showed him how to set the temperature.

"Now we just wait for it to beep, pop it in, and set the timer."

"Simple." Ronan smiled down at her. He was so close that she could feel the heat from his body. She stepped back toward the refrigerator and noticed a yellowed note on it. She read it out loud.

"'Ronan, don't forget that trash pick-up is Friday.' That's funny. Did you remember to take out the trash?"

Ronan gave a half-hearted grin and gently stroked a finger over the note. "My dad wrote that. That was my big chore when I was ten. He wrote that before he and my mom left on that trip. He was so sure that I'd forget to take out the trash that week. I haven't had the heart to take it down. Incidentally, I've never forgotten to take the trash out!"

Tears welled up in Juliette's eyes. Ronan looked at her, concerned.

"Hey, I wasn't trying to make you upset, Jewels."

She quickly wiped her eyes and smiled, "No, you didn't make me upset. I just hurt for you, that's all."

"Well, that's crazy! I'm fine. I'm excellent." He sounded as if he was trying to convince himself as much as he was trying to convince her.

Fortunately, the oven beeped at that moment. She heaved a sigh of relief.

"That's it, pop it in!" She motioned for him to do it.

"Oh, right."

She showed him how to set the timer.

"As soon as that starts beeping, take it out and enjoy! Let me know how it tastes." She grabbed her purse.

I better get out of here. I can barely control my feelings as it is.

Ronan frowned at her. "Aren't you going to eat with me?"

"Well, I figured you and your brother could have a meal together."

"Sounds great." Mike's voice came from behind them. "What're you making?"

85

Juliette smiled as nicely as she could. Mike did *not* share Ronan's looks. He was tall, but pudgy and unkempt. He had a thick light brown beard that hadn't been tended to in months and looked as if it might have scraps of old food in it, and she was sure he was quite intoxicated. She would never have pictured these two as brothers.

"Hi, I'm Juliette." She extended her hand.

"Well, hello, Juliette. I'm Mike." He took her hand, kissed it, and slowly eyed her from head to toe until her skin crawled. "You have stepped up your game, Ronan."

Ronan turned red. She had never seen him blush before. He pulled Mike's hand away from the firm grasp he had on her and pulled him into the living room. She heard him sternly say, "Go back to bed. I'll wake you up when the food is ready."

"It was nice to meet you, Juliette!" Mike sang as he stumbled to his bedroom.

"Your brother is nice," she said politely.

"He is a horror show," Ronan said under his breath. "Stay and eat with me. I don't want to eat alone."

Juliette blinked. This situation didn't seem right, but it wasn't right for him to be alone either.

Why do his darn eyes have to be so blue?

"We can watch something - whatever you want. It won't be weird, I promise. Just two friends who are hanging out and eating dinner. Come on."

"Okay, but just for a little bit."

She chose a light sitcom, which they both loved. She curled up in an armchair on the opposite side of the room, wanting to keep a safe distance from him. Ronan was right; it wasn't weird at all. It was as if they did this all the time. They even laughed at the same parts of the show. After they had finished eating, he made popcorn and convinced her to stay through "one more show", which then turned into three, followed up with a popcorn throwing contest, which she naturally won.

"Hey can I ask you something? It's been bugging me," Ronan asked as he stretched his long legs across the couch.

"Sure. Shoot."

"Don't get pissed, I just really want know. Why are you with Todd?"

She was sure her face showed her shock, because he followed quickly with, "Never mind. It's none of my business. It's just…"

"Just what?"

"You could do so much better than him."

Juliette laughed. "What do you mean? Todd is a great guy."

"Juliette, you are gorgeous, smart, funny, cool."

The temperature of the room escalated with each word.

"It doesn't seem like he gets how special you are."

She threw a pillow at him. "Stop it already! Todd has character, and I respect him."

Ronan made a face of disgust.

"Well, what about you? Why are you with Samantha?"

"First of all, I'm not with Samantha. Let's clear that up right now." He waved his hand emphatically.

"What is she then?"

"Just a friend."

"Oh, just a friend? Like me?" She was enjoying watching him squirm.

He leaned forward, resting his biceps on his knees. He looked at her intently, his eyes pulling her in. The feel of his lips flashed in her memory, forcing her to catch her breath.

"Nothing like you," he whispered.

They watched each other from across the room. Juliette's heart raced with anticipation and anxiety.

"I have to go," she heard herself say.

Ronan stood. "Stay."

Juliette tore her eyes away and made long strides toward the front door before she could change her mind. "Look, my mom sent me over here to drop off a casserole *three hours ago*! I'm lucky she hasn't called the police."

Ronan smiled at her. She cocked her head.

"What? Do you think I'm a sheltered little girl?"

He thrust his hands deep into his jeans pockets and looked at the ground. "No. I think it's nice. Appreciate what you have, Jewels. It can all change so fast."

A wave of empathy ached to her soul, and she instinctively threw her arms around his neck in a tight hug.

88

"I'm so sorry, Ronan," she whispered in his ear. Before he had a chance to respond, she dropped her arms and turned to go. "I'll see you on Monday," she called as she raced to the car.

What is wrong with you, Juliette! She thought as she climbed in her mom's beat up car.

She turned and waved, and he did the same. A flush of warmth surged through her. It was unsettling how addictive this sense of rapture was becoming.

Chapter 20

Ronan

RONAN SHUT THE FRONT DOOR and slowly walked back to the couch. He continued to watch tv, but his mind was on Juliette - on her small body, her soft voice, and the genuine kindness and compassion in her tawny eyes. Every baby hair that framed her face was calling to his lips, every slight curve of her body was begging to be touched. It had taken an extraordinary amount of willpower to keep his aching hands to himself. The way Juliette bashfully tucked her hair behind her ears, looking up at him beneath her long lashes, it was maddening. If he had thought that for one moment she would reciprocate, it would have been a done deal. He wanted to teach her every carnal pleasure that she had been denied. Up to this point, he had been curious and confused as to what to do with her. Now it was clear. He wanted her for himself. He just needed to figure out a way to make that happen.

Chapter 21
Juliette

JULIETTE SAT ON HER LIVING ROOM FLOOR while Todd strummed through the same chords for the tenth time. He came over on Sunday evenings to practice playing and get her opinions on his music. It usually turned into more of a private concert. Juliette enjoyed it. She loved to sing, and Todd was talented at writing music. As they sat on her living room floor that Sunday, she found herself studying him in ways she hadn't before. He was looking over a song he had written for them to sing together.

"No, that would sound better in G minor..." he mumbled to himself and pulled a pencil from behind his ear, scribbling on a piece of paper on his knee. He did have a nice jaw line, and the ways he pursed his lips when he was deep in thought was adorable. She wondered what it would be like to kiss him.

Juliette sat right next to him, her legs crossed, with her head on her hand.

"Todd?"

"Hm?" he answered without shifting his gaze away from his paper.

"Why haven't we kissed yet?"

That snapped him into attention. He stared at her with eyebrows raised. "What?"

Juliette let out a heavy sigh. "I know we've talked about being careful, it's just you haven't even tried making a move. Aren't you attracted to me?"

Todd guffawed, "Juliette you are being absurd. Where is this coming from?"

"I've just been thinking a lot lately. I think we should try it."

Todd dropped his eyes and scrambled through his papers. "We're supposed to be practicing right now."

"I know, but I want to talk about this. We've been together for almost a year. I don't think this is normal."

"Well it depends on your definition of normal. What I found most attractive about you is your integrity."

Juliette clenched her jaw. "My integrity?"

"Yes. It's what I'm looking for in a wife." He stared at her long and hard. She was suddenly afraid he could read her thoughts. "Why are you bringing this up now, Juliette? Is something going on that we need to talk about?"

She shrugged. "I guess I'm feeling a little unsettled. Maybe we should try things we haven't tried and see what happens. How do we even know we're compatible?"

Todd's face reddened. "Compatible?"

"Just listen to me, Ronan -," she stopped herself too late. They stared at each other aghast.

"What did you just call me?" Todd's voice was low and deep. Almost like a growl.

"I'm sorry! I've just been tutoring him lately. It just slipped out. It has nothing to do with this conversation."

"Oh, I think it very much does." Todd gathered his papers briskly and thrust his guitar in its case. "I think we're done here."

"Where are you going? I want to talk to you about this. This is important." Tears were welling up in her eyes, making her furious. She wanted to be in control of her emotions for once.

Todd threw his guitar case over his shoulder. "Listen Juliette, I'm not going to change. When I'm ready to kiss someone, I will. Until then, I won't. I told you when we got together that I don't want any distractions from my relationship with God, and *you* said you felt the same way. I waited a long time before I asked you out, because I wanted to be sure. I watched you and I waited until I knew it was right. I take all of that very seriously. I'm sorry that you don't feel the same way. I guess maybe it means we're not 'compatible.'" His signature sarcasm rang through his last sentence. He grabbed his keys off the coffee table and turned his back to her. "I'm going to Lois's. She gives real feedback on my songwriting, and she doesn't nag me about things I'm not comfortable with. See you tomorrow."

She didn't bother stopping him. She jolted as he slammed the front door shut. "See ya," she said sadly to the air.

Chapter 22

Juliette

JULIETTE FLUCTUATED between defeat, guilt, and anger all through the following week at school. Todd refused to acknowledge her in gym on Tuesday *and* Thursday, the one class they shared together, and wouldn't so much as answer her texts. At the end of the day on Friday, Ronan approached her as she was packing up at her locker.

"Hey," he sang, as cheerful as ever.

"Hey," she snipped.

"Sheesh what did I do?"

"It's not you." She glared at Todd who was packing his backpack halfway down the hall, acting as if she didn't exist.

Ronan whistled. "Trouble in paradise?" She sensed sarcasm in his tone.

"Not today, okay?"

"Okay, sorry. How about I take you out and cheer you up?"

"I really don't think that's going to help my current situation," she replied. "Besides, I've got this BBQ tonight at Pastor Vick's."

"I don't have plans tonight. I'll go and keep you company."

Juliette considered his offer. It would be nice to be around someone with a pleasant attitude for the evening. Ronan watched her with puppy eyes. She didn't want to hurt his feelings. "It starts at 6:30. I'll text you the address."

"Great. See you there," he said way too loudly and walked down the hall, right past Todd.

Todd stared hard at her from the end of the hall and slammed his locker shut. She pursed her lips together and returned the glare until he spun on his heels and stormed down the hall.

That evening, Juliette stared at her closet for a good ten minutes before choosing an outfit. She wasn't sure who she was dressing for, so she decided to dress for herself. She picked her favorite pair of jeans, her plainest flannel button up, and her most comfortable boots. She threw her hair into an easy ponytail.

Whatever happens tonight, happens.

She was tired of walking on eggshells for Todd's sake.

Ronan was already at Pastor Vick's, standing in the driveway, when she drove up with Lois. She hadn't told Lois that she had invited him, and before they got out Lois raised her eyebrows at her, "Girl, you are full of surprises these days. What are you up to?"

"Why does everyone assume I'm up to something? I'm just living my life. Maybe people should stop thinking they've got me all figured out."

Lois glared at her.

Juliette let out an exasperated sigh. "Sorry. I'm just upset over that stupid fight with Todd, and Ronan makes me feel better."

A large smile spread across Lois's face. "Honey, you've got it bad. Come on."

Lois opened the door and got out before Juliette could protest.

Ronan beamed a glorious grin, "About time you girls got here. I didn't want to just bust into some random party."

"Don't be silly," Lois responded, her voice oozing with congeniality. "We're all friends here. Right, Juliette?"

"Right," Juliette responded, instantly wanting to leave. She crossed her arms over her baggy flannel, which suddenly seemed very frumpy.

Ronan leaned in and whispered, "You look really cute."

Her cheeks flushed and a smile creeped onto her face against her will. "Thanks."

The awkward evening was becoming more uncomfortable with every passing minute. Todd arrived soon after she and Ronan had sat down with hotdogs and she felt his eyes watching her every move. Ronan, who seemed completely unfazed, never seemed to stop talking.

What was I thinking?

She didn't have anyone to blame, she had created this situation for herself. Lois sat next to Todd and kept grinning at Juliette as if this was some joke that she was thoroughly enjoying.

Some help you are, she thought as she sent mental daggers at her "best friend."

"Hey, are you okay?" Ronan asked, bringing her back to reality.

"What now? I'm sorry I zoned out," she replied.

What a weak response.

"I just need to use the bathroom real quick. Sorry." She hopped up and hurried in the house, leaving a rather confused-looking Ronan sitting behind on a camp chair.

She shut the door to the bathroom and took in a deep breath.

What is wrong with you?

She stared at herself in the mirror, not recognizing the person she saw. Her actions these days were completely off script. It was like she was acting in a play that someone else had written. Or maybe this was the real Juliette?

Ugh no. Get it together.

She turned the faucet on and flushed her face with cold water. It wasn't long before she heard the doorknob rattling.

"Just a minute please!" She said a little too sharply.

"Oh, sorry!"

She looked in the mirror again. "You can't hide in here forever," she whispered. "Go out there and deal with your problems."

She stepped out of the bathroom with confidence and walked to where Ronan was standing next to a freshly made bonfire, putting marshmallows on a stick. He looked at her with knit brows.

"Hey are you alright?"

"Actually Ronan I-"

"Juliette?" Todd's voiced interrupted her from behind.

She spun around startled. "What?"

"Can I talk to you for a minute?" Todd asked softly.

"Yeah." She turned to Ronan. "I'll be right back."

She followed Todd to the front yard, leaving Ronan holding a stick in one hand and a handful of marshmallows in the other.

Chapter 23

Ronan

RONAN HUFFED AND SAT BACK DOWN in the camp chair.

What am I even doing here?

Juliette obviously had no interest in hanging out with him tonight, and he didn't know anyone else here other than Lois and Todd. There was no way in hell he was talking to them. He threw the marshmallows in the fire in aggravation and rose to leave.

"Hey, do you mind if I sit here?" Pastor Vick sat down before Ronan could respond. He was wearing cargo shorts, a ratty t-shirt, flip-flops and a baseball cap with unruly wisps of blonde hair sticking out. If it weren't for him holding a sleeping infant on his shoulder, he could have passed for a high school student.

"Sure I guess. I don't think Juliette is coming back."

Pastor Vick nodded. "Yeah, she seems a little preoccupied tonight."

Ronan sat back down. "For real. I don't know why she even invited me."

"Sorry, man. Girls are complicated," Pastor Vick shrugged.

Ronan laughed. "You are so right about that."

He felt oddly comfortable sitting with Pastor Vick. The associate pastor, Pastor Al, had greeted him earlier, but the conversation was forced and insincere. At least that's how Ronan took it.

"Hey do you mind if I ask you something?" Ronan asked.

"Shoot," Pastor Vick responded.

"Why did you move to this hell-hole?"

99

Pastor Vick threw his head back and laughed loudly, causing the infant on his shoulder to stir.

"Sorry that came out wrong. I really just want to know."

"Naw, it's a fair question. Prepare yourself, it's a long story."

"I've obviously got nothing else to do," Ronan said.

"I was born in Maine. My parents were drug addicts, so my life was pretty unpredictable. I was in and out of foster care through elementary and middle school. When I was about to start my freshman year of high school, my dad overdosed. My mom was in jail at the time, and my grandparents had walked away from us a few years prior, so I was officially up for adoption. The thing is, no one wants a scrappy 15-year-old who's failing every class and constantly getting in fights. Needless to say, I never got adopted. It was rare for me to be in the same house for more than a few months, so I changed schools a lot. My senior year was the worst. I had decided that I was going to kill myself. I just hadn't decided exactly how I was going to do it. Before I could figure it out, this kid in one of my classes invited me to church. I have no idea why I decided to go, but somehow I ended up there and-" he choked up, causing him to pause, and stared into the fire. He cleared his throat and continued, "I found Jesus. That's the only way to describe it. A thousand pounds lifted from my chest in one night. I was free."

He looked Ronan in the eyes. "I knew I had to help other people out of that death swamp, so I went to Bible school. I learned everything I could, just tore it up. I think every professor on my campus knew me by name." He smiled broadly. "And that's where I met Felicia." He looked at his wife across the yard. She was a thick Latina with satiny black hair. She was laughing hysterically at something one of the teenage girls had said.

"And now I've got this little squirt here." He gently kissed the infant's head. "I've been given so much, more than I could have dreamed of. You know, there's a verse in Joel that says 'I will restore to you the years the locust has eaten', and that's exactly what God's done for me." He looked at Ronan as if he was peering into his soul. "I'm here to help people like you find the right way too, Ronan."

Ronan had been entranced in his story, fixated. Pastor Vick's heavy gaze brought him back to reality and he shifted uncomfortably in his seat. "Well my life is a wreck. Hopefully one day I'll have a comeback story too."

Ronan stared at his hands. He wasn't ready to spill his guts the way Pastor Vick just had. He wouldn't even know where to begin.

Pastor Vick didn't pry. They sat in silence together, watching the flames lick the sky. Ronan felt that same lump rising in his throat that had threatened tears at the youth group meeting.

"Hey, man, I'm gonna take off." He rose to his feet and started walking away, but stopped and turned.

"It was cool talking to you." He meant it. Pastor Vick had entrusted him so much personal information, he felt undeserving.

"You too, Ronan." Pastor Vick gave him a gentle smile.

Ronan walked to his car, but Pastor Vick called after him, "Hey Ronan!"

Ronan turned and Pastor Vick said, "You'll never have peace until you make your peace with God. If you ever want to talk again, I'm always available."

Ronan didn't have a response, so he merely stared back. He turned and briskly walked to his car. He'd had about all he could take for one night.

Chapter 24

Juliette

TODD LED JULIETTE to the front yard by hand and paused in front of his jeep. Juliette tried to stifle the anxiety rising in her chest.

"What is it, Todd?" She spoke slowly and carefully. She couldn't afford another name mishap.

Todd studied his shoes carefully. "I've been thinking over our conversation, and I think I owe you an apology."

Juliette's brows shot up. This was unprecedented. "Really?"

Todd stared past her, avoiding eye contact. He shifted from one foot to another. "Maybe you're right, you know? It's my own personal rule to wait until I'm engaged to kiss, but I shouldn't force that on you."

He stepped toward her until they were chin to chin.

Juliette's eyes popped open and her muscles tensed.

Surely he isn't-

Before she could complete the thought, Todd lunged forward and pressed his lips hard on hers. He gave her a stiff, forced kiss. His lips were cold and wet, Juliette felt her stomach recoil. She couldn't will herself to return it. After a few seconds Todd pulled away, and they stared at each other, inches apart.

Juliette couldn't formulate words. She had brought this upon herself, so there was nothing to do but face the consequences that were literally staring at her, inches from her face. Her displeasure must have been apparent on her face, because Todd stepped back, furrowed his brows and cocked his head.

"Is this not what you wanted?"

"Yes. I mean, no." She covered her face with her hands. "I don't know what I want."

"I'm sick of your games," Todd's voice was thick with agitation.

She heard the crunch of rocks beneath his feet as he walked away. She waited until he was gone to open her eyes and let out a puff of air. She stared into the black night, horrified at the turn of events this evening. She saw Lois appear slowly in darkness.

"Come on kid, I'll take you home," she said in a motherly tone.

Juliette didn't bother responding, but followed her like a downcast puppy to her car.

Later that evening she stared at her phone. She owed Ronan some type of explanation. She had completely ditched him. After texting out a few apologies and promptly erasing them, she decided to call.

"Yo," he answered.

Well, at least he doesn't sound angry.

"Hey, Ronan. I called to apologize." She lay back into her pillow, readying herself for a fight.

She heard him sigh on the other end. "It's fine. You have stuff going on. You don't need to explain."

"Wow, I'm impressed. This is super mature of you," she teased.

"Well, I am a really mature type of guy, Miss Monte," he said flirtatiously.

Juliette suppressed a smile and bit her lip. "It's ok to be mad at me, Ronan. I was a real jerk tonight."

"Well I guess it just made me realize how I've acted towards some people myself. It didn't feel too great, to be honest. Don't worry though, I'm coming up with some ways that you can make up for it."

"Oh boy. You just let me know when you decide on my punishment."

"Don't you worry your pretty little head about that, payback is coming," he laughed.

Juliette flipped onto her stomach. She could easily spend all night talking to him, but it was better to shut it down now before they got carried away, again.

"Hey, I'm pretty tired. I'll talk to you later, ok?"

"Putting me off again. I see how it is."

"I'm not, Ronan!"

"Mmhm. Goodnight, Princess."

Her stomach whirled inside of her.

"Goodnight," she replied and quickly hung up.

She tried desperately to sleep but found herself tossing for what seemed like hours, trying to force her mind to stop thinking about her horribly awkward kiss with Todd, while also steering thoughts away from a boy with twinkling blue eyes, deep dimples, and lovely full lips.

Chapter 25
Juliette

JULIETTE HAD A LOUSY WEEKEND. Todd had sent her the dreaded "let's take a break" text Saturday morning. He gave her the silent treatment through Saturday and Sunday, despite her multiple attempts to call and text. She hated the thought that she had caused someone pain, and the feeling that she was disappointing someone, but she couldn't reconcile a way to bring peace to this situation. She tried distracting herself on Sunday after church, but her usual go-to books weren't capturing her attention today. She scrolled through pictures of her and Todd on her phone, suddenly wondering if they had ever actually been happy together.

Everything was fine in my life until I kissed Ronan, she kept thinking. How could one little kiss throw her entire world off-kilter? She had been perfectly satisfied with her small life, even if she was at times frustrated with Todd. He was never mean to her, and they generally had fun together. After Todd had kissed her, the realization was sinking in that they didn't seem to have any chemistry. At least it was nothing like what she felt when she was with Ronan.

Why didn't I see this before?

Todd had a powerful way of putting guilt trips on her, and usually it worked, but each day that he played his games sent new waves of resentment through her.

Can't even handle one argument. What a coward, she thought in disgust.

Lois was acting as mediator, and she was enjoying this role thoroughly. She spent all Sunday afternoon at Todd's house talking to him. Juliette jumped when Lois finally called her.

"Sorry, girly, it's a no go. He's still pissed."

Juliette sighed. "I figured as much. He's being such a baby. I'm sorry you wasted your whole day talking to him," Juliette said, realizing it was now after 8pm.

"Oh, I didn't mind," Lois laughed nervously, "Todd and I understand each other in ways that you two can't."

Juliette was dumbfounded. *What does that mean?* Before she could answer, Lois quickly changed the subject.

"But if you want to return the favor, I need your help tomorrow. I completely forgot that I agreed to put together a photo montage for prom. You've got that nice camera your dad gave you. Could you walk around tomorrow and take pictures? The deadline to submit is May 20th. I only have three days, and my camera sucks. Do me a solid?"

Juliette agreed and began first thing Monday morning. She tingled with nostalgia as she walked through the halls snapping pictures of people. There were so many people that she hadn't spoken to in her entire four years as a student at Avalon High. Her personal goal as a student was to keep her head down and get through it. She didn't want to get caught up in any shenanigans. She wanted to be a good example. Now she was realizing that she'd been so successful at being a wallflower that she hadn't made any impression at all. Had she shared her faith with even one student here? She couldn't pinpoint one. She'd been to every Friday night youth group meeting, but other than Ronan, she couldn't think of a single person she'd ever invited to go with her.

What have I been doing all this time?

She felt a weight increasingly wearing her down throughout the day as she moseyed around the halls snapping pictures of people. Lovely people, many of whom she'd never see again after June 19th. When the bell rang at the end of the day, she exited the back way and walked to the pool building. She could catch the swim team practicing. She fought back tears as she sauntered through the doors.

I'm sorry for wasting so many opportunities, Lord. Forgive me.

When she walked in, she was disappointed to find that only Ronan and Dre' were there. "I thought you guys usually had practice after school. I was going to get some last minute pictures for the prom montage. Where is everyone?"

Ronan swam to the edge where she was standing. "Well, our big meet was last week, so no one cares much anymore. Dre' and I are just keeping our form. You know, we both got scholarships." He was beaming.

Juliette smiled. "I know you told me. That's so amazing. Congrats, Dre'."

"Thanks! I don't know if I'll take it. I don't think my mom's gonna let me go to school in Texas." Ronan frowned at him.

"Didn't you tell her I was going too?"

Dre' nodded. "That's part of the problem. You got a reputation in this town, my friend. Mom doesn't think I should be going to college with a party animal."

"I'm not even like that anymore," he said as he pulled himself out of the pool and dried off. Juliette gulped hard and averted her eyes from his beautiful glistening body.

"Anyways, I'm just here for the pictures. Can I grab one of you two?"

"Absolutely!" Ronan grabbed Dre' by the neck and gave him a noogie. Juliette laughed and snapped a picture.

"Hey, don't put that in! You gotta make me look good." Dre' stood as tall as he could and gave a huge smile with his perfect white teeth. Ronan smiled, and his gorgeous dimples stood out. They were quite stunning together. This picture would be a hit; she was sure of that. After she snapped the picture, Dre' grabbed his bag.

"I'm off. Laters." He gave Ronan a fist bump and headed out. "Adios, Juliette."

"Oh, see ya later. I should go to." Her mouth went dry.

"No. Stay," Ronan said to her as he sat on the edge of the pool with his legs in the water. He draped his towel around his shoulders. His dark wet hair somehow looked perfect. He patted the cement next to him. The whole scenario looked dangerous to her. She didn't know if she'd have the self-control to keep her hands to herself if she spent a moment sitting next to his sleek body.

"Just for a minute. I won't bite," he grinned.

But I might, she thought.

She sighed. He was irresistible. She walked over, took her flip flops off, and dipped her legs in the water. Today was the first day it was above 50 degrees, so naturally she wore shorts and flip flops. She paired it with an oversized hoodie, though. She wasn't trying to get too crazy.

They sat in silence for a moment. It was peaceful. Sitting in silence together didn't feel awkward anymore.

"Your brother is a lot older than you, isn't he?" Juliette asked. She'd been curious about the situation with his brother but wasn't quite sure how to broach the subject.

Ronan nodded. "Yeah. I was an accident. Or as my parents called it, a 'surprise.' They only meant to have him, but you can't stop this." He pointed both thumbs to his chest.

Juliette smiled and rolled her eyes in response. "My little brother was a 'surprise' too. Mom's doctor said she couldn't have anymore. And then came Markus! Wild as can be." She laughed.

"Well, at least he's cool. My brother is terrible," Ronan said, bitterness thick in his voice.

There was no sense in arguing about it, he did seem awful. "Was he always like that?"

Ronan sighed heavily. "No. Well, he was always a jackass. He was Mr. Perfect in high school. Straight As, amazing basketball player. He had just finished his first year at Georgetown University when my parents died. Then he

110

just gave up everything; his future, his dreams, and even his girlfriend who was his whole life. He was just gone."

He had a faraway look in his eyes as he talked. Juliette resisted the urge to hug him. She didn't want to make that mistake again. And it probably wouldn't end well with him being half dressed and them being alone. She placed her hand on his shoulder instead.

"I'm sorry, Ronan. That must be so hard. Almost like losing him, too." She said quietly.

"I did lose him," his voice quivered. "This scholarship is my chance to get away and start over. It's my only chance."

Juliette shook her head. "I can't imagine what I'd be like if I had to go through all that you have."

Ronan looked down at her with his lovely blue eyes. His eyelashes looked incredibly long when they were wet.

"You would be okay, Jewels. You're strong." He leaned against his hands, every muscle in his chest and abdomen was chiseled to perfection.

"So, what's going on with you and Todd?" He asked, staring at the pool.

She eyed him cautiously. "We're on 'break.'"

He chuckled. "You mean you broke up."

"No, not totally. Not officially."

He cocked his head at her. "Well, I wish you would."

She smiled slowly. "Let me take your picture."

Before he could answer, she snapped it. She wanted to remember this moment.

"Hey! Not fair. Now take one of us together."

He put his hand around her waist and pulled her close to him. She didn't bother resisting, but eased into him and snapped the picture. He looked over her shoulder, and they looked at the picture together. To anyone else looking at it, they would have looked like the world's most content and happy couple. Juliette noted how dreamy she looked and how blissfully happy Ronan's smile was.

"Beautiful," he whispered in her ear, sending shivers down her spine. She knew she should move, but her limbs were frozen in this moment. Ronan gently brushed her hair off of her shoulder and lightly kissed her neck. She caught her breath and her toes curled against the edge of the pool.

"Ronan, don't," she barely managed to say.

He didn't answer, but laced his fingers in her hair and focused on her neck.

If he kisses me one more time... Now she knew she better get out quick. She hopped up. "Want to grab a coffee?"

Ronan shook his head and sighed. "If that means I can be with you, then sure. I'll get coffee. Just give me a minute to get dressed."

Juliette went outside to wait. She realized she was shivering, but not from the cold. Why was it so easy to be with Ronan? They couldn't be any more different, and yet somehow, it seemed like God pulled their souls from the same stardust.

Chapter 26

Ronan

RONAN SAT ON HIS COUCH THAT AFTERNOON and contentedly cracked open a can of coke. He didn't necessarily have a plan with Juliette, but things were developing naturally, and for once, he didn't feel pressured to force anything. It was easy, comfortable. Before he could take a sip, he was startled by the doorbell. No one ever rang the doorbell here. Every friend that stopped by walked right in. He suspiciously looked through the peephole half expecting the police to be there with an arrest warrant for Mike, but was equally shocked to find Lois Cabana standing on the porch. He slowly and suspiciously opened it.

"Um, can I help you?"

Lois's arms were crossed. She didn't look happy. "Yes, you can," she answered, and pushed past him. She walked directly into the living room and sat on the couch like she owned the place.

"Have a seat, Casanova."

Ronan slowly walked to the living room and sat across from her. She didn't immediately speak, just eyed him up and down, taking him in with a frown.

"I assume you're eventually going to tell me what's going on here?"

Lois took a deep breath. "That's funny. I came here so that you could tell me what's going on." She paused and narrowed her eyes. "You know that I'm Juliette's best friend, right?"

Ronan nodded.

Lois leaned forward with her arms crossed. "She told me she kissed you on the field trip, Ronan."

Ronan smiled. "Is that right?" He proudly sat down in the recliner across from her and spread his arms like a king on this throne. "What exactly did she tell you?"

"She told me it was nice."

Ronan thought his face might split from smiling so hard, but he couldn't stop himself. "You don't say?"

"And now she's been spending all of this time with you. When I ask her about it, she insists you're just friends, but please. I've known Juliette for ten years. She can't fool me. So are you two together and hiding it, or what?"

Ronan leaned back into the couch. He thought about what he should answer for a moment. He settled on the truth. "We're not together."

"Then what is going on?"

He shrugged, not bothering to hide his disappointment. "Nothing is going on."

Lois sighed heavily. "Listen, Ronan. I'm going to be perfectly honest with you. I think you're probably a decent guy, despite your awful reputation."

"Gee, thanks."

"I think you and Juliette complement each other. I think Todd and Juliette are wrong for each other, I've always thought that. And that isn't because I don't like Todd, he's one of my best friends. Todd and Juliette just don't belong together, and now that they are on break, it's your opportunity to make a move."

"So you really want your two best friends to break up? That seems weird. What's in this for you?"

Lois was silent and shifted uncomfortably. "I have my own reasons."

Ronan huffed. "That's vague."

"That's all I want to say about it. I'm going with my gut here, but just to be clear, what are you intentions with Jewels? Are they honorable?"

Ronan thought about that. *Honorable?* That was an interesting word. He'd be lying if he said all his thoughts about Juliette had been "honorable." It would be more accurate to say that he wanted to corrupt her; but it was more than just that. This wasn't a game to him. He thought differently about Juliette than he had about any other girl.

"I want to be with her." It came out before he'd even finished thinking it through. "Well, what I mean is..." he looked around the room. It felt odd saying it out loud. As if he was telling a secret. There was no way out of this now. He sighed heavily.

"I know what you, and probably everyone else, thinks about me. I feel different about her, though, and I would treat her right. She's not like anyone else I know. She's warm, and kind, and funny... and so many other things I can't even find the words for. When I'm with her, it feels like there's a chance I'm not just a piece of crap wasting his life away. She makes me feel like I matter. I know it's crazy, but I want her to be my girlfriend. Do you think that could happen?"

Lois smiled for the first time. "Maybe. It's a long shot."

"Well, what can I do?"

Lois laced her hands together over her knees. "I have an idea. If we work together, I think we can make it happen."

Chapter 27

Juliette

JULIETTE HAD GOTTEN TICKETS TO SEE HER FAVORITE BAND, Middle Chapter, for Christmas. The anticipation of going to New York City with Lois for an entire day, on their own, was thrilling. She had only been there with her family, so she was limited as to what she could do. She and Lois had carefully mapped out their day with places to go and things they would eat before the show started at 8 pm. New York City was about two hours from her, and her parents had agreed to a late curfew, just this once. She excitedly packed her backpack that Saturday morning with snacks and headed downstairs for breakfast.

"Hey, mom! Do I look like a tourist?" She twirled. She knew she looked amazing. She just wanted to hear it. She had put this outfit together a few months ago: an oversized sweater, black leggings with a leather mini skirt, and tan booties.

"That skirt is as little short." Her dad bristled as he sipped his coffee.

"Her skirt is fine!" Her mother snapped at her father, then she turned to her with knit brows. "Honey, I need to tell you something." Her mom's tone concerned her.

"Mom! You can't change your mind now. I told you I would be careful."

"No, that's not it. Lois is sick. She can't go."

Juliette's jaw dropped. "That can't be true. I just talked to her last night!"

"It happened overnight, some stomach bug. She called this morning, didn't want to upset you. She had a great suggestion, though."

Juliette plopped onto the stool, deflated. "Yeah, right. Like what?"

"She suggested that Ronan Richland go instead. He'll be here in fifteen minutes." She casually sipped her coffee.

Juliette's heart dropped to her feet.

"This can't be real. Mom. I can't go with him!" She pleaded.

"Why not? Your dad talked to him on the phone. He promised he would take good care of you and drive carefully, and he's been on the Subway many times, so you won't get lost."

"And you trust him? You barely know him! You guys have always been so strict. What is happening here?"

"I trust *you*, Juliette. You're eighteen now. You're always telling us to lighten up, so we are."

Juliette's mouth gaped open. She glanced desperately at her father. He was frowning, his large arms folded across his gut.

He doesn't look happy.

"Dad, are you ok with this?"

He sighed heavily. "Not entirely. Your mother has been talking me into it all morning." He scowled at her mother. "I've heard some rumors about this boy that caused me some concern."

"Please! Do you remember how you were in high school? 'Mr. Bad Boy', and look at what a softie you turned out to be!" Her mother playfully poked him in the ribs. He gave one of his hearty laughs.

Gross.

"Todd will freak when he hears about this," she said to herself. She hadn't told her parent's about 'the break.'

Her dad chimed in, as if reading her thoughts. "I thought about calling Todd, but he's with his dad for the weekend to tour Boston College. Besides, you know he wouldn't be any fun." Her dad had never like Todd. He thought Todd was arrogant and disrespectful to Juliette. Even so, she couldn't believe he would be okay with her taking a day trip with a boy he'd never met.

He really is putting a lot of faith in me, she thought.

Her father rose and kissed her on the head. "I would go with you, hun, but I've got to get on the road now." He smiled at her sweetly. "I know that you are a good girl," he said as he headed out the door.

Juliette gulped hard and stared after him.

Her mom leaned over and took her hands. "Juliette, if you don't want him to go with you, we can cancel. I will not let you go alone, though. Is there anyone else you can think of to go with you?"

Sadly, she could not. There were some girls she occasionally hung out with from youth group but spending the entire day with them sounded like torture. Being with Ronan that long would be painful in a different way.

"No Mom, it's fine. He's a good guy. We'll have fun." Her mom frowned. Juliette chuckled and said, "Not too much fun."

She headed back up to her room.

Fifteen minutes…

She contemplated changing. She checked every aspect of her image. She didn't think she could look better than this. Her hair was flowing in soft waves. Her makeup was on point.

Ronan is lucky that he gets to spend the day with someone this cute.

She laughed at the thought. The doorbell rang, tying her stomach in knots. She wondered if she should call and ask Todd's permission. It was a little late now if he did say no.

He is in no position to grant me permission anyways, she thought as she walked out of her room.

Ronan smiled up at her. "Ready?"

He looked like he had rolled out of bed and thrown on some jeans and a hoodie. In other words, he looked perfect.

How annoying.

"I'm ready." She smiled back, threw on her backpack, and turned to kiss her mother goodbye.

"Please don't make me regret this," her mom whispered in her ear.

"I won't." She winked at her mom as she headed out the door.

Ronan's car smelled especially fresh and looked a little cleaner than usual as she climbed in. She threw her backpack in the back seat.

"Thanks for doing this, Ronan. I can't believe Lois bailed on me. She was fine yesterday!"

Ronan shrugged his shoulders. "Well, you know how stomach bugs are. They come out of nowhere. She sounded pretty miserable on the phone." He seemed to be avoiding her eyes.

Juliette squinted her eyes at him. "So when exactly did she call you? Why would she call you and not me?"

"I don't know, Jewels. She didn't want you to be disappointed? Anyway, forget about it. We're gonna have a great day." He looked at her and flashed a glorious smile. She decided she'd drop it for now.

"Fine." She eased back into her seat as he pulled out of the driveway.

"What kind of snacks you got back there? Give me some."

"We just left, Ronan! These are for the whole day!" She laughed as she dragged her backpack into her lap.

They laughed and listened to music the entire ride there. Ronan had never heard of the band, so they played nearly all of their songs, and he loved it. As far as she could tell, he was telling the truth.

"So what's the first thing on this list of yours for the day? Hopefully food. I'm starving."

"Well, you ate *all* of our snacks already so I guess we can park and catch the subway to Queens. There's a great little dive there. Do you like Chinese food?"

He smiled at her. "Jewels, I love all the foods."

She laughed back at him. She doubted she would be having a better time with Lois.

They parked his car at Yonkers Station and walked toward the terminal.

"Let me see this list you made."

He read it slowly as they waited on the train. He laughed when he got toward the bottom.

"Museum of Natural History? Is this a fifth-grade field trip?"

She snatched the list away from him in aggravation. "Well most of this was for me and Lois. Do you like to shop?"

Ronan scrunched his nose.

"I didn't think so. I don't really know what to do then," she sighed

"Chunk the list. Let's just have fun." He winked at her, sending her heart into flutters.

Usually, this would give her anxiety, but she fully trusted Ronan and felt safe going wherever he chose to lead. She crumpled the list and tossed in a trash can.

"Lead the way," she smiled.

Chapter 28

Juliette

THE AIR WAS CRISP and there was a light breeze as they stepped off the Subway in Queens. The temperature was perfect, but the wind carried a chill, so Juliette was grateful for her sweater.

"Where to?" Juliette questioned.

"Well, there's this cool neighborhood I want to check out that has a ton of graffiti in it. Do you mind walking?"

"Of course not, I've got all day. Let's go!"

Ronan grinned and grabbed her hand, lacing his fingers through hers. His touch warmed her from her toes up, and took the chill out of the air. They walked along the busy city streets slowly, allowing the feel of New York to settle in. People bustled past them with no regard, so set on their destinations that they didn't seem to notice two wild-eyed teens. The graffiti was bright and inviting, a startling contrast from the flat concrete streets and buildings. Juliette snapped dozens of photos with her dad's camera. She wanted to be able to savor this trip later on. They walked through a 99-cent store and Ronan bought her a fake red rose. She tucked it in her purse and mentally told the butterflies in her stomach to simmer down.

Ronan convinced her to eat lunch at a sketchy looking deli she wouldn't dared to have set foot in without him. As it turned out, they made the best cheeseburger she'd ever had. As they leaned against the brick on the outside of the deli, Juliette studied Ronan's stunning profile. His thick dark hair had a cowlick on the side that she had never noticed. He was scarfing down a cheesesteak as if he was in some kind of eating contest. He looked back at her as he licked his fingers clean.

"What?" he asked, sounding a bit self-conscious.

"I'm just thinking how I wouldn't be doing any of this if I weren't hanging out with you," Juliette replied.

"Is that a bad thing? We're having fun, right?"

"Yeah, it's great. Take a picture with me."

Ronan didn't hesitate, but pulled her in and kissed her on the cheek as she snapped the picture. She playfully pushed him away. "I didn't tell you to do all of *that* now," she laughed.

"Sorry. You smell like a cheeseburger, it made me hungry." He winked at her, making her smolder. "Come on, let's keep walking."

They came upon a Chinese market and spent a couple of hours sampling authentic Chinese food. Juliette would have balked at eating diced rabbit in bone marrow soup a couple of weeks ago, but Ronan's coaxing turned out to be quite convincing. They found an open art studio and discovered that neither of them had any understanding or appreciation of modern art. They bought matching t-shirts at a flea market, and blew $20 worth of quarters at an arcade.

As the day wore on, she became more aware of a feeling of liberation. Something that had been stifled inside of her was awakening. Juliette forgot about the concert altogether.

"Hey what time are we supposed to be at that show?" Ronan brought her back to earth.

"Oh, shoot." She glanced at her watch. "It starts in half an hour!"

He smiled down at her. "You're so cute. 'Shoot'… ha! I'll get us there. Don't worry."

Ronan hailed a taxi immediately and comfortably settled in the back seat. They got to the venue with two minutes to spare. Ronan winked and jumped out to hold the door of the taxi open for her. As they walked in, he rested his hand on the small of her back. She didn't stop him. She liked the idea that they looked like a couple walking in. The venue was relatively large, but it was standing room only. He walked them over to the side of the room, pulled her close to him, wrapping his arms around her waist. Her gut told her that she was leading him on, but she didn't have the gumption to pull away. He felt like a warm blanket. He rested his chin on the top of her head as the band began playing a mellow song.

"Hey, I don't know if I told you, but you look really pretty today," Ronan leaned in and whispered in her ear.

Juliette's insides turned liquid. "You told me." She thought about telling him how dreamy his eyes looked, how strong and capable his arms felt around her waist, but an internal voice told her to be careful. She bit her lip and leaned into his embrace. He buried his face in her hair and inhaled deeply. He didn't say anything else, for which she was grateful. If he whirled her around and kissed her, she'd lose herself to him completely. They stood suspended for the next couple of hours, as the band played all of her favorite songs.

Chapter 29

Ronan

THE TRAFFIC WAS BRUTAL when they finally got to Ronan's car.

"I'm going to be so late for curfew," Juliette moaned. "Dad will never let me out again."

"I'll get you home safe and sound. Relax."

He whipped out onto the road without a thought. He didn't seem phased by the aggressive drivers around them. At first, Juliette clutched the sides of her seat as he was driving, but began to relax after a few minutes.

"You are an excellent driver," she said as she settled into her seat.

"You seem surprised."

"You just don't seem like the type I guess."

"Well, when both your parents die in a fiery car crash, you tend to pay attention when you're driving."

Juliette's eyes nearly popped out of her head.

"Well, that and I have this sweet BMW to take care of, which apparently cost a lot of my parent's inheritance." He chuckled to himself.

"Ronan, I am so sorry! I wasn't trying to be insensitive."

"Psh obviously I know that. Chill out! I'm just teasing you." He reached over and ruffled her hair. She pulled his hand off and the feel of her skin sent small shockwaves through his core. He considered holding her hand again, but withdrew and gripped the steering wheel. He couldn't focus on the road if he was touching her.

Juliette fell asleep thirty minutes into the car ride home, leaving Ronan alone in the quiet with his thoughts. Usually, he had the radio going to avoid these moments, but he didn't want to wake her. She was sleeping so peacefully, she looked like an angel. By all accounts, this had been a perfect day. The best day he could recollect in his life. Holding her through the show had been an almost unbearable tease. The entire time he thought about when they had kissed, how red her cheeks and been and how full her lips were. His pulse was rising with each passing minute. He was so confident that she was something that he wanted, but the further he dove into these feelings, the more terrifying they became. She had lit a fire that he could not contain.

As he pulled into her driveway, he thought about Lois's words. "*If I'm going to lie to my best friend and miss an awesome show, you better at least kiss her.*" He gently nudged Juliette awake.

"Wake up, sleeping beauty." He whispered gently.

"Are we here already? I'm so sorry. I only meant to take a catnap."

"You say sorry for the weirdest things. Don't apologize for everything, Monte." He smiled and winked at her.

As they slowly walked up to the steps, his stomach churned. Would she reject him if he tried to kiss her? Technically she still had a boyfriend, and her convictions were strong.

"Are you alright? Did you have fun?" She looked at him with furrowed brows.

"Of course. I had a great time. Why do you ask?"

"You're just so solemn looking. It's making me worry." She smiled at him gently.

"I've just got a lot on my mind lately. What about you?"

"I had an amazing time." She smiled. Her hair and eyes seem to be glowing in the moonlight.

He looked at her a long time on the front steps, contemplating. Worrying about making a move was a new feeling. She didn't budge from his gaze, and he felt like she was pulling him in somehow. His eyes shifted to her incredible full lips, but the moment before he plucked up the courage to make a move the light flickered on in the foyer, snapping them back to reality.

"Goodnight, Juliette." He leaned in, hugged her lightly, and walked away.

"Goodnight, Ronan." She called after him softly.

He cursed himself as he drove home. He had chickened out. On the other hand, he felt some relief. This ambiguous friendship wasn't some flirtatious little fling to him. It felt delicate - as if one careless move would dissolve every possibility of a future with her. Dread overcame him as he pulled into his driveway and saw Samantha sitting on his front porch, looking furious.

He slammed his door shut and walked up to the steps. Samantha was the last person he wanted to deal with at the moment.

"What are you doing here, Samantha? It's 1 am." His voice echoed his irritation.

"A few weeks ago you would have loved to see me show up at 1 am." Her voice was shaking with anger. "So where have you been all night?"

He stared at her, wondering if he should be honest.

"You don't have to look at me like that, Ronan. I already know you've found someone else."

"Someone else? Samantha, for the last time, we were never together. We were having fun, that's it."

"Oh, and now you're done with me? Have fun with me and toss me aside like trash afterward?" Her lips were trembling now. "Are you and Juliette together?"

"What does it matter to you?! I don't owe you anything!"

She stepped forward and slapped him so hard in the face that his ear started ringing.

"You will soon find out how much you owe me." She stormed off and left before he could respond.

Ronan trudged into his house, flopped on his bed and covered his face with a pillow, defeated.

What did I get myself into?

Samantha was right; a few weeks ago, his life made sense. He knew exactly where his future was going. Perhaps his reputation was flawed, but that wouldn't matter for long. Now he was going to church and spending the day with Juliette Monte?

What is happening?

His face was still stinging horribly. No doubt he had a big print on his cheek from Samantha's substantial hand. What had he ever seen in her exactly? Any guy who was hooking up with her didn't deserve to be with Juliette Monte.

"Mom, I wish I could talk to you..." he whispered in the dark. He fell into a restless sleep imagining what his mother would say if she could see him now.

Chapter 30
Juliette

JULIETTE STOOD AT HER LOCKER AT THE END OF THE DAY on Monday when Samantha strolled up. Juliette had noticed Samantha glaring at her frequently that day, and she assumed it had something to do with Ronan. She refused to entertain it. With her wild red hair and hard black eyeliner, Samantha could be quite frightening. Samantha towered over her now with a forced smile. Finally, she spoke.

"Hi, Juliette! I wanted to congratulate you on being Ronan Richland's latest conquest!" Her voice boomed. Everyone's eyes turned in their direction.

Juliette wanted to disappear. She couldn't cover Samantha's mouth, not unless she wanted to get her lights punched out.

"Samantha, I have no idea what you are talking about." She carefully steadied her voice.

"I think you know what I'm talking about. Masquerading around here, acting like you have a boyfriend and then sleeping with Ronan on the side. Fake people like you make me sick."

A crowd was gathering around now. Juliette could feel the fury creeping through her arteries and into her cheeks. "You don't know what you are talking about so I suggest you zip it."

Samantha didn't break her gaze for a moment. "Don't worry, precious innocent little dove. I won't get in your way. I just came to give you a gift."

She flung a box of condoms hard at Juliette's head. The crowd around them went wild with "damn!" and "oh snap!" Juliette wished the earth would swallow her whole.

"You'll be needing these. Ronan has quite the libido, and I wouldn't want you getting pregnant. Good luck to the two of you!"

She turned on her heels and walked away, leaving Juliette holding a box of condoms and a small bruise forming on her temple.

Juliette froze. Hot tears were forming in her eyes, but she refused to cry in front of her classmates. When she was able to move, she took quick steps to the closest trashcan and threw the box in. The crowd descended like vultures to a corpse to collect them. She took the opportunity to dodge into the girl's locker room and collapsed onto the nearest bench. She sobbed into her hands.

I did this to myself.

She had let herself believe that she was innocent, and that this was just a friendship, but her feelings had betrayed her.

I am such a fool.

Of course, Ronan had slept around. She knew his reputation. And she had a boyfriend! How was this fair to Todd? Had she lost all sense of morality? The locker room door opened, and Ronan stepped in.

Juliette quickly wiped the tears and snot from her face into her cardigan.

"This is the girl's room. You aren't supposed to be in here," she said as she looked up at him.

"I heard what Samantha did. I'm so sorry. She's completely insane." He seemed truly concerned.

Juliette looked at the floor. "Don't worry about it. It's nothing."

"It's not 'nothing', Jewels. You didn't do anything to deserve that."

He sat next to her on the bench quietly. Juliette's balled her hands in tight fists, forcing herself to remain in control.

"Samantha thinks that she and I have a relationship, but we don't. I'll make sure she never talks to you again." His voice was soft but firm.

"What she said though, it made me think…" Juliette paused.

Ronan looked at her anxiously. "Think what?" he asked quietly.

"Maybe we shouldn't be hanging out so much."

Ronan shook his head. "We haven't done anything wrong, Juliette. Why should you care what someone like her thinks?"

"It's not just her. Todd is still refusing to talk to me. He probably thinks the worst of me now. I don't want people thinking I'm just another…." She stopped herself.

"Just another girl I'm sleeping with." Ronan finished her sentence. She looked him in the eyes. His beautiful, ocean blue eyes.

"I'm not as disgusting as you think, Juliette."

"I didn't say that you were."

133

"I don't want you to walk away over something like this. Getting to know you the last few weeks has changed my whole mindset. I don't want to lose you."

He sounded desperate. He grabbed Juliette's hand and laced his fingers through hers.

"I feel different about you. I know that sounds cliché. I mean it, though. I want to show you that I'm a good guy. I can make you happy if you let me. We have so much chemistry. There's something special between us and I want to see where it goes." His voice broke at the end of the sentence as if he was straining to say the words.

Juliette had a firestorm of emotions running through her. She couldn't think of what to say. She just stared at his hand, holding hers.

"You should break up with Todd, and go out with me."

That snapped her out of it. "What did you say?"

"You guys obviously aren't right together, Jewels. You should be with me. I will be good to you, I swear."

"You and I cannot be together, Ronan," Juliette said this as matter-of-factly as she could.

"Why?" He sounded angry.

"We don't have the same moral values, Ronan! It won't work!"

"How do you know if you don't try?" He was raising his voice now. She dropped his hand.

"It just won't! God is the priority in my life, and He's not even a thought to you! I can't work with that! And you are moving to Texas in a few months. Tell me how that would work exactly?"

Ronan looked furious now. He stood, and she lost some of her gumption as he looked down on her.

"So I'm just some immoral piece of trash to you? Were you hanging out with me because you felt sorry for me or something?"

She stood and tried to meet his gaze. "No Ronan. That is not what I meant at all. Don't put words into my mouth."

He raised his hand to stop her. "I know what you meant."

He stormed out of the locker room and slammed the door behind him. Juliette stood stunned. She thought about running after him but remembered the crowd of vultures who were no doubt right outside the door. Plopping back down on the bench, she ran her fingers through her white-blonde hair.

"What a disaster," she whispered to herself.

Chapter 31

Ronan

RONAN WAS SO ANGRY he couldn't focus on where he was driving. He didn't want to go home, and the pool was locked. Cruising around town aimlessly, he eventually wound up at Dre's house. He wasn't even sure he would be home when he knocked on the door. Unfortunately, Dre's mother answered. She pursed her lips together when she saw him.

"Good afternoon, Miss Walker. Is Dre' home?"

"He's in his room. I'll let him know you're here," she said coolly. "You can come in."

She left him waiting in the foyer. *She hates me. I guess there's no chance he'll be coming to Texas.* He pushed his hands deep into his pockets. He wondered if everyone thought he was the scum of the Earth.

"Hey, man! Wassup?" Dre' walked up and smacked his shoulder. "Come to my room!"

Dre's mother whispered something in his ear and glared at Ronan. He wanted to pull his pockets inside out and say, "Look! No drugs!" but thought better of it. He smiled at her instead as he walked past her down the hall.

Dre' shut the door behind him and flung himself on a beanbag near a TV where he'd been playing a video game. "To what do I owe this pleasure?" he asked with his huge smile.

Ronan slunk into a beanbag near his and sighed heavily. "I don't know. I didn't know where else to go."

Dre' furrowed his brow. "You alright, man? You're not your usual chipper self."

Ronan explained what happened. "I don't get her. We have this obvious chemistry. She's flirting with me one minute, and the next I'm not good enough for her? What am I supposed to think?"

"Huh," Dre' said, linking his fingers behind his head and leaning back in his beanbag. He was quiet for a few moments and stared at the ceiling, deep in thought. Finally, he spoke. "I dunno, man. I think you're being pretty hard on her."

"Seriously?"

"Look at things from her perspective, dude. A month ago, you were sleeping with Samantha, and who knows who else. Suddenly you're interested in her, and she's supposed to throw herself at your feet?"

"I never said that. I said I thought we should give it a try."

"But you don't see how she'd be hesitant?"

Ronan bit his lip hard and his brow tightened. His thoughts spun with this new perspective, he couldn't grasp onto a worthy rebuttal.

"Let's say you did start dating. Juliette said God is the most important thing in her life. Do you think she's gonna sleep with you?"

"I can wait."

"Yeah but how long? Juliette's the kind of girl that waits until she's married. Is that what you want?"

Ronan wrinkled his nose. Marriage was nowhere on his radar.

"Plus she's right -you're leaving. Do you want to have a long distance relationship right when you go to school? I thought you said you were never coming back here?"

"Ok fine! I get it!" Ronan stood up.

"Where are you going?"

"To apologize. For being a jerk."

"Maybe you should give her a little space. Remember you aren't her boyfriend."

That hurt.

"Yeah, I know. Jewels made that clear. Maybe I'll call?"

"Text."

Ronan sighed. "Deal."

Dre' settled deep into his beanbag. "Why don't you play me on this? It would get your mind off of it."

Ronan stared at the screen. Some first-person shooter outer space game. "Um, no. Not my thing at all. I'll chill with you and watch. I'm not in the mood to go home yet." He sat back in the beanbag.

Dre' smiled. "Great. It's taco night at my house!"

"I'm sure your mom will be thrilled to have me," Ronan said sarcastically under his breath.

Chapter 32

Juliette

JULIETTE PULLED INTO TODD'S DRIVEWAY and turned the ignition off. After she'd had a good cry in the girl's locker room, she regrouped and figured out what to do next. She was lost when it came to Ronan, but she knew what she needed to do with Todd. They needed to break up, officially. He was working on his Jeep, his one true love, in the driveway and turned to her covered in grease.

"Well, it's now or never," she said to herself and got out.

"Hey," she said meekly.

"Hey," he returned coldly.

"We need to talk."

He stared at her blankly for a few moments. "I expected this," he said matter-of-factly. He laid whatever tool he was holding down and crossed his arms.

"Say what you came to say."

Juliette swallowed hard. "I think we should break up," she said quietly.

After a long cold stare from Todd, he answered, "And why is that?"

Todd had a way of making her feel like a terrible person, like the world's worst sinner. It was so hard to read his emotions. She was always guessing at what he was thinking. At first, it made him seem mysterious. Now it was just plain aggravating.

"Because we aren't right for each other."

"And this wouldn't have anything to do with Ronan Richland, would it?"

"What? No! We should have broken up a long time ago. We aren't in love – so what are we doing? There's no reason to keep this going. We've barely even talked the last two weeks."

"That's because you've been avoiding me."

"And you haven't been avoiding me?"

"*Fine.*" Todd rarely raised his voice. It startled Juliette, and she jumped back a little. "It's over. That's what you wanted, and you got it. Don't come complaining to me when Ronan gets you pregnant or gives you some STD."

"Wow. You are such a jerk. I can't believe it took me this long to realize it." She felt hot tears well up in her eyes.

"Then why are you still hanging around here?! Leave already!"

Tears stung Juliette's eyes and made it hard for her to see. "I'm leaving! It's a shame it's come to this after a year together."

"This is all on you, Juliette." He turned and started working on his Jeep again.

He couldn't care less about me. I am such a fool.

Juliette drove home in a flood of tears. When she burst through the door, her parents were sitting in the living room. They looked at her, alarmed.

"I broke up with Todd," she managed to say before a new watershed of tears burst forth.

"Well it's about time," her dad said soothingly and pulled her into a bear hug.

Chapter 33

Juliette

AFTER A GOOD CRY and pep talk from her parents, Juliette felt slightly better. She had been mostly worried about what her mother would say, but it was an unfounded fear.

"Honey, Todd's mom and I have been friends for a hundred years. This won't change a thing for us. I hope you don't think I was expecting some kind of arranged marriage. I want you to be happy." Her mother gave her a soothing kiss on the forehead. "Besides, Ronan seems more like your type, if he's anything like his dad was," she said with a wink.

Her father groaned loudly.

"Oh, hush you!" Her mother threw a sofa pillow at him.

"I want ice cweem!" Markus shouted.

"Son, you are so wise. How about you and Mommy go to the store and get Juliette some rocky road?" She gave Juliette a little smile.

"Yeth!" Her brother whooped excitedly.

"Be back in a jiff!" Her mom said as she grabbed the keys and headed out the door.

There was an awkward silence left in the room, where she and her father sat opposite each other. He cleared his throat and opened the coffee table drawer, pulling out a purple folder.

"Now that we're alone," he said, "I want to talk to you about something."

Juliette sucked her breath in. "Oh boy."

"Don't worry. It's nothing bad. This is actually the perfect opportunity." He sat next to her.

"Listen, your mom is hell bent on throwing you in the arms of another boy, but I want other things for you." He stared hard at the folder in his lap. "You're too good to be in someone else's shadow. Lois, Todd, and now maybe this new kid, who I'm not real convinced on. You need to figure life out for yourself, without these overbearing people. You've got so much to offer." He teared up.

"Dad! I already cried a ton tonight. Don't make me cry more," Juliette warned.

"Ok. I'll suck it up. Anyway, you know your mom and I can't help much with college. I wish we could. But we can afford this." He handed her the folder.

She opened it and skimmed through the contents. There were pictures of beautiful forests, mixed with pictures of people being baptized and feeding children in third world countries. The front of the brochure read "YWAM North Cascades. From the Pacific Northwest to the Ends of the Earth."

"Okay, Dad, I'm lost here."

"This is something Pastor Vick showed me. It's a missions school."

She kept her perplexed look.

"It's only six months, you'll get a little Bible school training and then you'll go on a missions trip. Then you can come home and start classes at the community college here in the spring. I think this is perfect for you, hon. You'll get a bigger picture of the world, and maybe figure out what you are supposed to do in this life." He took her hands in his. "I really, really don't want you jumping into another relationship. You're nobody's sidekick. This is a once in a lifetime type of opportunity. Promise me you'll think about this. If it's something you're interested in, I can talk mom into it."

"Okay, Dad. I promise." She was overwhelmed with the love in his voice, and gave him a hug. "I love you, Dad."

"Love you, too."

Late that night she got a text from Ronan. "Sorry, for being a complete jerk. Please forgive me."

She didn't reply. She hadn't told her parents what had happened at school with Samantha and Ronan, and she never would. She would never be able to look her father in the eye and tell him that story. It would break his heart. She closed her eyes and drifted off to sleep. Today had been exhausting, but somehow she felt a sense of relief.

Chapter 34

Ronan

RONAN WRESTLED WITH HIS EMOTIONS through the week. Juliette had texted him back on Tuesday evening with a brief, "don't worry about it, Richland". He couldn't think of a response. Everything he thought of saying sounded psychotic. She was obviously avoiding him at school, and it was making him physically ill. He didn't even have an appetite anymore. He knew he should let this girl go, but couldn't bring himself to do it. He nearly called her a hundred times through the week, and even drove past her house once. He was worried that he might be turning into an obsessive stalker.

Her words kept rolling through his head, "God isn't even a thought to you." She wasn't wrong. Ronan spent no time thinking about God. When his parents had died, Mike was furious at God. He refused to even talk about going to church. It was bizarre not to go after they had gone faithfully every Sunday for years. Ronan couldn't say that he'd ever felt angry at God, nor was he an atheist. He didn't see how God cared about what happened to people. If He did, why had he gone through all that he'd gone through? Where exactly had God been the last eight years? How was he supposed to make God a priority when God hadn't even noticed him when he needed Him the most? The more Ronan thought about it, the more frustrating it was. What was this girl thinking? She was banking all her happiness on some celestial being that didn't care about her at all. It was almost comical, but then he remembered how she looked when she sang. Her aura almost pulsated into the gloom surrounding him, it was magnetizing. He wanted to be there with her, glowing. On Sunday morning, he decided to do something entirely out of his element. He got up and went to church.

He recognized many faces when he walked in. They were just a little older. People looked at him curiously and greeted him, but they didn't seem to recognize him, for which he was grateful. He didn't resemble either of his parents, so he wasn't surprised they didn't know him. He saw Juliette in the front, but lost courage and slunk into a seat in the back before the service started. He'd never felt more uncomfortable in his life. He wore a polo and khakis for one, which he loathed. Looking around now, he noticed that most people were in jeans. He wondered why his parents had always made him dress up for church.

The service began with an older gentleman asking everyone to stand and sing. The band on stage started an upbeat song and a group of people in front of them sang with their eyes closed. Unfortunately, Juliette was not on the stage. More unfortunately, Todd was. He spotted Ronan right away and gave him a look to kill. Ronan thought seriously about leaving but realized this would only bring more attention to him; that and he couldn't let Todd win. He was officially stuck here now. The service was interesting. The sermon was about being real and honest when praying to God, bringing everything to him. The idea of being authentic with God was a new concept to Ronan. Could he talk to God like a friend? He packed it away to ruminate on later. For a while, he was so captivated that he forgot why he'd even come. As soon as the service ended, he remembered. Juliette stood and froze when she saw him. She was wearing an adorable red summer dress that accentuated her soft curves. He took a deep breath and then made strides toward her. Her father joined her side as soon as he reached her. He was as tall as Ronan, and quite intimidating with a shock of orange hair. Juliette was still wide eyed, clutching her Bible to her chest as if for protection.

"Hi, Ronan," she said quietly.

"Hey, Juliette," he responded. He instantly forgot everything he had planned on saying to her when he looked into her big chestnut eyes.

Her dad looked from Ronan's face to Juliette's as they stared at each other silently. Finally, he stuck his hand toward Ronan. "Hi! I'm Juliette's father, Mully. I don't believe we've met?"

Ronan took his hand and gave it a firm shake. This was a man he needed to make a good impression on. "Hi, Mr. Monte. I'm Ronan Richland. We talked on the phone last week."

His eyes narrowed, taking him in, and his lips coiled into a skeptical smile. "Ronan Richland! We finally meet again. Gracious, you've grown! It's great to see you!"

He grabbed Ronan into a big bear hug. Ronan was dumbfounded. He couldn't remember the last time anyone had hugged him that way. It was terrifying, but kind of nice as well. He awkwardly hugged him back.

"Dad! Let him go! You're probably freaking him out!" Juliette turned to Ronan. "Sorry, Ronan. I'll walk you to your car."

"It was nice to see you again, Ronan!" Her dad called after them in a booming voice, causing several heads to turn.

They quietly walked to the car, with many curious eyes following them. When they finally got there, Juliette broke the silence.

"I didn't text anything else because I wasn't sure what to say. I'm sorry. I shouldn't have said all of those things to you. I promise I wasn't trying to say it in a mean way. I don't think you're a bad person. You're awesome! I'm sad it took until we almost graduated to find that out."

He could tell she was being earnest. He wanted to pull her in and cover her with a thousand kisses. She was right about one thing; they had wasted so much time. He sat three seats away from her last year in Biology and had probably spoken less than two sentences to her the entire time. Where would they be now if he had made the effort to have just one conversation with her? He could kick himself.

"I was the wrong one, Juliette. Your friendship means a lot to me. I hope you can forgive me and we can still be friends."

Juliette smiled. "Yes. Friends."

Ronan took a step toward her. "So, can we still hang out then?"

"I don't see why not."

"What are you doing right now?"

Juliette smiled adorably. "I got a job. At the Steam Stop. I'm going to be a barista!" She put her hand on her hip and posed.

He overcame another strong urge to kiss her. This girl was turning him inside out.

"Wow, that's awesome. You can get me some discounts. I'll be in to see you for sure."

She laughed. "Okay, you do that. I have to go now. I can't be late for my first shift! See you later!"

She got on her tippy toes and gave him a quick kiss on the cheek, then turned as red as her dress and hopped in her mom's car. Ronan's stomach did somersaults as she sped out of the church lot.

"Bye," he said to the dust haze she left behind, his head quite literally in the clouds.

"Good job, Romeo!" Lois's roaring voice startled him from behind, effectively snapping him back.

"What?"

"Well, whatever you are doing is working. Although I'm pretty sure you have a lifelong enemy in Todd now."

"What do you mean?"

"They broke up, you dummy."

Ronan stared at her until this turn of events sunk in. A smile spread slowly across his face. "Is that right?"

Lois punched him hard in the arm. "Yes, it's right, you crazy fool. Juliette told me a little bit about what happened between you two. She's falling for you despite herself."

She pointed her finger at him and narrowed her eyes. "I'm only breaking her confidence right now for her benefit, so if you decide to screw her over, I will *kill* you."

"You don't have to worry about that. If I get a half a chance with her, I'll treat her like a goddess."

Lois cracked a smile. "Right answer."

Juliette was becoming the focus of his whole being. He wouldn't do anything to jeopardize that.

Chapter 35

Juliette

JULIETTE GOT A TEXT during her shift from Lois saying "come to my house when you're done. Urgent." She rolled her eyes at it.

Always so dramatic.

Her first shift was busy and a bit overwhelming -who knew there were so many possible coffee combinations? The shift started at 1pm and didn't end until well after 9pm; she didn't think she could take what would surely be several hours of Lois's chatter only to be up again at 6am for school the next day. She called her from her car.

Lois answered after one ring. "Hey girl, are you on your way?"

"I just got in my car. Is this something that can wait until tomorrow? I'm beat."

"No, I would rather talk to you tonight. It won't take long," she said firmly, quite different from her usual theatrical tone.

"You're making me worry now. Is everything ok?"

"Sure. It will be. See you soon," she said as she clicked off the phone call.

"Well I guess I don't have a choice now," Juliette said wearily to herself as she started her car. This week had drained her of emotion, she wasn't sure she could bring herself to react to another crisis.

She pulled into Lois's driveway and found her sitting on her front porch with her arms crossed, eyebrows knit in either worry or resolve. It was hard to tell. Juliette approached her cautiously and scrambled her brain to pinpoint any way she may have pissed Lois off. Lois could be overly sensitive at times, but nothing overt was coming to mind.

"Have a seat, kid."

"You know I'm older than you," Juliette teased in response, but Lois stared straight ahead without smiling. "Alrighty then," she sighed and sat next to Lois obediently, "what's up?"

Lois took a deep breath. "I haven't been exactly honest with you." She took a suspense filled pause, Juliette forced herself to wait patiently. "I may have had ulterior motives in wanting you and Todd to break up."

She paused again. This time Juliette didn't have the fortitude to wait. "I don't follow. What do you mean exactly?"

"Well, besides just thinking that you and Todd are wrong for each other, which I totally do, I wanted you to break up with him for my own reasons." She shifted a bit and turned to face Juliette. "I like him."

Juliette's jaw dropped. "Come again?"

Lois sat up straighter and repeated, "I like him."

A deafening silence suspended in the inches of space between them.

"Lois, I don't even know what to say."

"There's nothing to say, I just wanted to be honest with you. I haven't done anything wrong, so I'm not apologizing. I just wanted you to know that I plan on going after him."

"Going after him? It hasn't even been a week since we broke up! Don't you think that's going to be a little uncomfortable for me?"

Lois clenched her hands and responded, "Maybe so, but as your best friend, you should think about how I feel in this situation. I've liked him for a while now, and I've had to sit around and watch you two have this terrible relationship when I know you're wrong for each other. I've been patient, and now it's my turn to be happy. I'm not asking for your permission."

Nausea crept into Juliette's throat. What was the right emotion to feel at this moment? Even if she could determine that, there was no way to identify anything she was feeling. Somewhere between disgust, betrayal, and outrage. She wanted to let loose on Lois, but the indignant determination in Lois's eyes made her catch her breath and think twice. If there was going to be a throw down, there wasn't a chance on this Earth that Juliette would win it.

"What do you even like about him? You see how he's treated me all this time. He's rude, and condescending, and judgmental. Why would you want that?"

"That's only because you don't understand him. He's a deep thinker, and an artist. We connect that way."

Juliette clenched her keys so tightly the pain vibrated up her forearm. "So, you're an artist now too? I guess there are a lot of things I don't know about you." She could sense her rage boiling over, so she stood.

"You said what you needed to. Best of luck to you both," Juliette said as angry tears stung her eyes. She took great strides to her car as Lois watched her. She took one more look at her before she drove away, hoping that this was some sadistic joke. Lois pursed her lips and stuck her chin in the air in response.

Juliette was so flustered on the way home, she couldn't formulate a plan on what she ought to do. The person she would typically call in this situation was now the betrayer! She sat in her driveway, unwilling to walk into the house. She didn't want to burden her parents with yet another one of her dilemmas. She decided to call Ronan and was grateful when he picked up with a cheerful, "Hey, Princess! How was your first shift?"

"I'd forgotten I even worked today. Let me tell you what just happened," she said as she settled into the seat of the car. Ronan listened patiently as she described every detail of the scene that she had just endured.

"Can you believe this, Ronan? The audacity of this girl. I feel like I don't even know her!"

"Huh."

"Is that your only response?" She laughed.

"Well, I'm not totally surprised. She did have her eye on him."

"What! When?"

"Pretty much every time they were together. I guess you were oblivious."

154

"Unbelievable," she said more to herself than to Ronan. Her mind raced through the last few months. Had she noticed anything? She was sure she hadn't, and yet the evidence must have been right in front of her face. She had spent the last month more worried about Ronan than anything that was going on with Todd or Lois. Maybe she was the bad friend in this situation? The thought made her chest tighten.

"Try not to worry about it too much. I don't think Lois handled this the best way, but I do know that she cares about you," Ronan said soothingly.

Juliette smiled in the dark. He was doing a spectacular job of lifting her spirits.

"Thanks. I feel a little better now. I'll let you go. Sorry I called so late."

"Jewels, you can call me anytime, anywhere. I'll spend all night on the phone with you, if you want."

Juliette felt her face flush. "Thanks. I'll keep that in mind."

They said goodnight and hung up. She stared at her phone for a few minutes before walking into the house. What a bizarre turn of events this last month had brought her. Lois and Todd had faded into her background, and Ronan Richland, of all people, was becoming her closest confidant. She smiled to herself as she recollected his last remark to her. She'd gladly spend all night talking to him, too.

Chapter 36
Juliette

RONAN AND JULIETTE SPENT EVERY DAY TOGETHER over the next week. They used the excuse of 'studying to get Ronan to pass the Chemistry final', but they both knew that was a farce. Juliette and Lois hadn't exactly made up, but Juliette gave Lois placated approval to avoid any more confrontation. Lois had taken it and run, spending all of her time trying to woo Todd in his fragile, bruised-ego state. Juliette was grateful to have less of both of them in her life for the moment. She spent the majority of her time laughing, flirting, and watching shows on her couch with Ronan, who drove her home daily. She even threw in a few cooking lessons. It was becoming more and more challenging to be with him without wanting to be *with* him. Her mother kept hinting at wanting them to be together, to her father's dismay. Her little brother jumped for joy every time he saw Ronan, and ran into his arms. Everything seemed perfect, and yet she had a small nagging feeling telling her "not yet." Ronan didn't push the issue. It was quite evident to everyone that he was interested. Even their classmates openly teased them in the hallways, but Ronan would always laugh it off, being the perfect gentleman. On Thursday, as they were lounging on the couch in her living room, he asked her if she had a date to the prom, which was the following Friday.

"No. Todd would have been my date, but after we broke up, I just figured I wouldn't go." She looked down and played with the fringe of the couch pillow. "What about you?"

"Obviously, I have a date. I'm Ronan Richland," he said smugly.

Juliette felt her cheeks sizzle. "Oh? Who is it?"

"You." He leaned forward. "If you'll have me, of course."

Juliette bit her lip to stop herself from smiling like a fool. "I'll check my schedule and get back with you."

"Well you go ahead and do that, and let me know. I've already got our tickets, and my suit is ready, I need to pick out a bowtie to match you." He grinned at her.

"I'm wearing a white dress with teal beading. If I say yes, that is."

"You have a dress already? I thought you weren't going." He laughed and poked her gently in the ribs.

Later that night as she tried to fall asleep, Juliette wondered if he would try something at the prom. Every high school movie made it seem like this was the night to "lose your virginity." It seemed absurd considering practically every girl she knew in high school had already lost their virginity ages ago. Juliette had protected hers vehemently. She had always felt that she was born in the wrong generation. Modesty was not a quality that was highly valued at Avalon High. She had been teased at times for being an "uptight prude." Most of the time, she felt like an alien amongst her peers. It was her keen sense of conviction that kept her away from most social gatherings. People understood that about her now, and so they generally left her alone and stopped trying to get her "drunk" or "high" for fun. This situation was much different, however. For the first time, Juliette wondered if the temptation might be more than she could withstand.

Chapter 37
Ronan

RONAN WOULD NEVER HAVE THOUGHT he'd be excited about going to prom. Until a few weeks ago, he would not even have considered going. Dressing up in and of itself was out of the question for any occasion. Things were changing quickly for him, faster than he could process. His priorities were completely different these days; namely Juliette and how to get more of her. He knew it made no sense. She'd offered him nothing more than friendship. He recognized that he was in danger, but he couldn't stop himself. He was utterly head over heels for this girl.

By all accounts, it seemed to be going well. Ronan had won the favor of her best friend, her mother and brother, even her father was warming up to him. The only egg left to crack was Juliette herself, and she was a tough one. He could sense her armor chipping away slowly. She no longer stiffened when he got close to her. If he kept playing his cards right, he could break that barrier before the night was over. He had no long-term plan. He knew that school was ending in a couple of weeks and that by the end of summer, he would be halfway across the country, but it didn't matter. That hadn't been on his mind lately at all.

He rang on her doorbell to pick her up for the prom and adjusted his bowtie. His thick dark hair was slicked back. His tux was crisp and clean. He looked good, and he knew it. With Juliette on his arm, he would be invincible. She was the hottest girl at Avalon High. Some might say that Andrea Mathews was, but her large breasts and exaggerated features never did much for Ronan. Juliette was petite and ethereal. She'd fit perfectly wrapped up in his arms. He pushed the thought away before it got out of control, just in time, as her dad answered the door.

"Welcome!" her dad boomed and grabbed him into a bear hug. He hadn't quite gotten used to her boisterous family and awkwardly hugged back.

"Mully, get off this poor child! Hi, Ronan. You look so handsome! Juliette! Ronan is here," her mother yelled up the stairs.

Ronan wondered where Juliette got her quiet nature. Between her parents and little brother buzzing between his legs making airplane sounds, his anxiety level was increasing by the moment. It disappeared the moment he set eyes on her. She was radiant. She seemed to float down the stairs. Her hair flowed over her shoulders in ivory waves. Her two-piece dress fit her like a glove, with a bit of her midriff scandalously showing. He wanted to devour her.

"Pictures!" her mom yelled. Juliette rolled her eyes, but shouldered up to Ronan and smiled.

"You look amazing," he whispered into her ear.

"You're not so bad yourself." She smiled back. She smelled sweet and flowery, matching her aura. It was intoxicating. It was throwing his equilibrium off as he attempted to walk with her to his car.

Before he made it past the front door, her father pulled his arm and said in a voice low enough for only Ronan to hear, "You try anything with my baby, you're dead. Capiche?"

Ronan turned to face him terrified, but he simply smiled back and shouted, "Have fun you two!"

When they got in his car, Juliette looked at him, impressed. "It's clean! And it smells great!"

He grinned at her. "Only the best for M'lady - and I made a playlist for tonight, which you will love. It has all of your favorite bands on it."

Fortunately, they had just about the same taste in music. Her favorite song came on, and she looked over at him and laughed.

"Okay, okay. I'm impressed. Good job, Ronan."

He bowed to her. "Thank you." Tonight would be a good night.

Chapter 38

Juliette

JULIETTE's ANXIETY ROSE every moment that she clung to Ronan's arm. He looked incredible, and she was proud to be with him, but she couldn't stop her mind from racing. She tried playing different scenarios in her mind, to prepare herself for whatever might happen. She'd never felt this vulnerable and open to someone before; it was unnerving to say the least.

"Do you want to dance?" he asked as they walked in together. Juliette looked at the dance floor. Club music was playing, and her classmates were taking full advantage of grinding on each other.

"Please, no."

"Thank God." He smiled down to her. "We can wait until a slow song comes on."

Slow dancing?

Juliette could feel her cheeks get hot, and her pulse race. She couldn't understand what was making her so nervous, but she felt like hightailing it back home.

As if the situation wasn't uncomfortable enough, she spotted Lois hanging on Todd's arm across the room. They hadn't really spoken the last couple of weeks, so it was shocking to see Lois hanging on the arm of her ex-boyfriend. Lois had made unusual effort to accentuate her dark eyes and thick brown hair.

She wore a tight-fitting cream-colored A-line dress that hugged her many curves, which were usually covered in layers of clothing. Lois glanced at her momentarily, then laughed at something Todd said. Odd, she couldn't remember Todd saying anything funny since she'd known him. A wave of nausea overcame her.

"You okay?" Ronan looked concerned.

"Totally." She managed a smile, but her heart had dropped to her feet. She didn't think she could have a good time with Todd's judgmental eyes watching her every move paired with the palpable tension between her and Lois.

"You sure you're ok with them being here? I don't mind if we leave," Ronan said, seemingly reading her thoughts.

She thought about being alone, in the dark, with Ronan Richland looking like an absolute dream. She shivered.

"Let's stay," she said.

The Cure's "Lovesong" came on and the lights dimmed. Ronan seized the opportunity and grabbed Juliette's hand.

"Come on."

It seemed she couldn't escape the danger. He pulled her close, and she wrapped her hands around his neck without hesitating.

"Let's see if you can dance, Miss Monte."

She smiled slowly, warming to him. "I think you'll be satisfied."

He pulled her so close that her belly and chest pressed into his. It was exhilarating. She was unaware of anyone else in the room. His solemn eyes were hypnotizing her. After two songs, her legs had turned to jelly. She didn't think she'd be able to stand if he held her a moment longer.

She let out a sigh of relief when he said, "Let's take a break."

"Sounds good. Let's go for a walk."

They walked out of the gym and down the hall. He didn't let go of her hand, and she didn't make any effort to get away. They walked slowly and silently. When they had gotten away from everyone, he stopped and turned to her.

"Juliette, I can't take this anymore."

She backed away a step, hitting the locker behind her. Ronan stepped forward and wrapped his hands around her waist. His fingertips on her bare midriff sent electric shocks up her spine. She sucked her breath in.

"Ronan, what are you doing?" she whispered.

"Something I've been wanting to do for a long time."

He leaned in and pressed his lips hard against hers. She felt lightheaded, out of her body. He wasted no time in kissing her and pressing in closer and closer to her. It was happening so fast that she couldn't process if she wanted it or not. Her blood felt like lava pulsating through her body. She put her hands against his chest and pushed him back with all her might.

"Stop it, Ronan!"

He stared at her blankly. "Seriously?"

"What do you mean 'seriously?!' Of course, seriously! Back off!" she could hear her voice getting louder and louder, but she couldn't stop herself. Her throat was tightening with each moment that she stood this close to him, she suddenly felt panicked and out of control.

"Calm down! I wasn't trying to force myself on you. Honestly, I don't know what you want. You're sending me mixed signals."

She had tears in her eyes, which was making her furious.

"I just need some space." She said and suddenly took off in a flash.

Ronan stared after her, too stunned to move or speak. He looked utterly crestfallen, and she felt like a monster for it, but she couldn't stop herself from running.

She found the nearest exit and escaped. The cold evening air felt good; it calmed her down a bit. She closed her eyes and took a deep breath.

You're okay. You're okay.

But she wasn't okay. She wasn't sure what had caused her to lose it completely. Wasn't this what she wanted? But then he was so close that she could feel his heart beating against her chest, she had suddenly felt that she was losing all control. It was horrid. She knew that if she didn't run for it right then and there, she'd be powerless to stop herself, and who knew where the night would take them? She wanted to give herself to him completely, and she nearly had. The thought made her shiver, she wrapped her arms tightly around herself. In the corner of her eye she glimpsed movement in the shadows and realized she wasn't alone.

"Todd? Is that you? What are you doing out here?!"

Can this night get any worse?

Todd was leaning against the wall. He looked quite handsome in his tuxedo. "Shouldn't I be asking you that?"

"It felt stuffy in there. I needed some fresh air."

Todd nodded slowly. "Same."

Juliette laughed silently. "I guess we aren't very social people, are we?"

Todd smiled. "Nope. We always had that in common."

He turned to face her fully and dropped the smile. "Won't your date be looking for you? I'm sure this is a big night for you two," he said, his tone changing to sarcasm.

Juliette could feel her blood starting to boil. "Todd, I told you we are only friends."

"Why do you insist on keeping up this charade? No one is buying it."

"It isn't a charade, Todd! Why do *you* insist on insulting me constantly? You and I were together for a whole year, and you still think that I don't have any integrity? You think I don't know that Ronan just wants to sleep with me?!"

Todd's face turned red. "Juliette. Stop."

"No! You listen to me. I know how Ronan is, but I'm smarter than that. I have no interest in losing my virginity to some cheap high school prom hook-up!"

165

"Juliette!" Todd yelled over her and nodded for her to turn around. When she did, she saw Ronan standing directly behind her, his face a ghostly white. She instantly felt like throwing up.

Chapter 39
Ronan

JULIETTE LOOKED DESPERATE as she begged, "Ronan, wait."

But Ronan didn't wait. He took off before she had a chance to say another word. She tried to follow him, but she couldn't even come close to his speed. He was in his car and out of the parking lot in seconds. He had no idea where he was going, but a cold crushing pressure was collapsing his chest, as if he was choking. Thoughts were racing through his head a mile a minute, none of them coherent. It was pitch black out now, and he could barely make sense of where he was going through this pulverizing anxiety.

You are trash. She knows you're trash. Why would she think any different?

He clenched his jaw and turned the radio on.

You know you'll never be good enough, for her or anyone else.

He turned the radio as high as he could to drown out these thoughts, but it wasn't working.

Mom and Dad would be so ashamed of you.

He knew he couldn't drive much further without having a complete meltdown. He recognized a street, turned, and made his way to the last house on the corner. Marty Eldridge. Marty was an old friend of Mike's, one that had done a fair amount of damage in their lives. Party Marty, as he was called, could supply you with just about anything you could ask for. Before Ronan could second guess himself he turned the car off and flung the door open. He made long strides toward the front door and pounded on it, refusing to allow his mind to think.

"Look who the cat dragged in," Marty said as he answered the door. The stale, moldy smell of Marty's house wafted into Ronan's nostrils, turning his stomach. "If you're looking for Mike, I haven't seen him in a couple days."

"I'm not looking for Mike," Ronan said as he pushed past the gaunt, tattoo-covered man and into the dark house.

Marty looked him up and down. "Oh right. It's prom night. Time to get blitzed. Did you come alone?" He hissed and peered outside.

"Yeah, just me. I just don't want to feel or think anything. Whatever it takes."

He refused to think about consequences. He was engulfed in an ocean of hopelessness, and if he didn't find an escape soon, he would drown.

A serpentine smile spread across Marty's skeletal face. "I've got just the thing. Make yourself at home. I'll grab it for you."

Ronan slunk into a nearby sofa chair that was caked in filth. He didn't care. He squeezed his eyes shut, willing this night to be over. He felt Marty open his hand and slip two tiny pills in his palm.

"Looks like you got it bad, little man. This will set you right. It's-"

"Don't tell me what it is."

Ronan took a deep breath, threw them in his mouth and swallowed without asking any questions. He handed Marty a wad of cash.

"Alright. See you on the other side, brother," Marty snickered and walked out of the room, counting the bills with a huge grin.

Within twenty minutes Ronan felt his mind slipping into a euphoric blue oblivion.

Chapter 40

Juliette

JULIETTE HADN'T SLEPT AT ALL THAT NIGHT. She had let Todd and Lois drive her home after Ronan took off. Neither of them said a word to her the entire time. The humiliation of that drive coupled with the guilt of her betrayal left her a hollow, wretched shell. She couldn't even look at her parents. She held her hand to them when she walked in the door, said, "I do *not* want to talk about it," and ran to her room. She promptly ran to her bed and wept into her pillow until the wee hours of the morning. Her mother anxiously checked on her, brought her hot tea and rubbed her back, but she would not be consoled. Her mother went to bed around 11:30pm, leaving her alone with her thoughts. Juliette was initially engulfed with shame and self-loathing, but as the morning dragged on, she was overcome with an intensifying worry.

"Please just let me know you're okay," she pleaded to Ronan through text messages. She called him on and off for hours, with no response.

At 4am, Juliette snuck out the front door and drove past Ronan's house. His renowned red BMW wasn't there, so she drove around town aimlessly looking. She kept flashing to the deep sorrow and betrayal that she had seen in his lovely eyes, which had been so tender toward her just a few hours earlier. No apology would suffice. Her concern for his wellbeing grew into an anguish of her very soul, so she decided to head home and pray. There was nothing else that could be done.

She knelt by her bed and pleaded, "God, something isn't right. I don't know what it is, but You do. I've been a complete fool, but right now the thing that matters is Ronan. Please help him. Please let me know what to do."

Pastor Vick.

Juliette paused. "What the heck does that mean?" She sat for a few minutes, wondering if she was imagining things.

"Do you want me to call Pastor Vick? It's 6:15!"

No response.

"Ok. Well, here goes nothing," she said to herself as she dialed his number.

A groggy voice answered the phone, "Juliette, is this an emergency?"

"Maybe," she chewed her lip. "I don't know if you remember my friend, Ronan?"

"Yes. I've actually been praying for him a lot."

"Well, I think he's in trouble, and he won't answer my calls. Maybe he'll talk to you?"

She heard shuffling through the phone.

"Give me his number."

Chapter 41

Ronan

RONAN AWOKE with the force of someone hitting him in the head with a baseball bat. He painfully opened his eyes and peered around the gloomy room, confused.

Why am I wearing a tuxedo?

He tried wiping his sweaty palms on the sofa chair he was sitting in. The cheap fabric was yellowed with what he hoped was age. He was startled by a snort, and turned to see a stranger sleeping on a nearby couch.

He swore and sat forward as the world spun around him. Slowly the events of the prior evening dawned on him, as damning as the sun rising through the filthy windows. The stranger moaned and turned on his side. Ronan grabbed his keys off a side table and rose to his feet, like a mummy rising from a thousand years underground.

He made his way quietly to his car. Marty had delivered on his promise, he certainly hadn't felt anything for a few hours, but now his stomach churned in waves of nausea and shame.

He drove away cradling his head in his hands, mostly because it felt like it might roll off. He had almost made it home when he suddenly turned.

I can't go home.

How could he face Mike? He had judged him so many times, but it turns out they were exactly the same. A wave of remorse flowed through him. Is this the way his brother felt every day?

What hell.

He drove aimlessly through neighborhoods that weren't quite awake yet, and imagined happy families dreaming peacefully in their beds. He took side roads until he was finally out of town. Blackbirds chirped as the sun began to crest over the tall pines. He was struck with the stark contrast of this blissful morning and his own turbulent psyche.

Stupid birds. They might as well be laughing at me.

He recognized a back road and drove down it. It was a little fishing hole with a small dock that his dad used to take him to. He pulled the car over and staggered onto the pier. His head throbbed, and his throat ached for something to drink, but the real drought was in his soul. As Ronan stared into the murky water, he wanted nothing more than to disappear into that blackness, for the agony of this life to be over. There didn't seem to be a point to any of it. For the first time in his life, he wished he couldn't swim.

He took deep breaths of the cold morning air. He couldn't formulate a single thought, but he felt the whole of his existence caving in on him.

He looked up at the sky and cried, "Where are you?"

He had no idea who he was talking to; God, his mom, his dad; anyone who would listen.

"God, if you're out there, and you give a damn about me, now would be a pretty good time to show up," he seethed, his breath puffing tiny clouds into the frigid air.

Ronan was startled by his phone ringing.

Probably Juliette calling for the millionth time, he thought.

He wasn't ready to talk to her, but he pulled his phone from his pocket anyway. It wasn't a number that he recognized. He wondered briefly if she was tricking him by calling from another phone.

"What do you want?" He snapped.

"Hi Ronan, this is Pastor Vick, from New Life Church."

Ronan blinked hard, trying to make sense of Pastor Vick's words. "Why are you calling me?"

"Juliette called this morning, she thought you might be in trouble. I'm worried about you, too. Can I come talk to you?"

"I'm at Burton's fishing dock," he choked out.

"Great. I know where that is. Hang tight, I'm on my way."

Ronan hung up the phone and took in deep, ragged breaths. Tears blurred his vision. He didn't bother holding them back this time.

Hang tight. Help is on the way.

Chapter 42

Juliette

A T 8AM, THE PHONE RANG. It was Pastor Vick. Juliette answered with an anxious, "Hello?"

"Good morning, Juliette. I've just spent some time with your friend. I think he's ready to talk to you."

Juliette's heart raced. "Where is he?"

She threw some sweats on and was out the door in a flash. She didn't even bother checking her reflection in the mirror, knowing that she would be appalled at what she saw. That wasn't important. She needed to apologize as quickly as possible.

She was at the pier in minutes. Ronan sat on the edge, staring at the water. She caught her breath and slowly walked towards him, her legs growing heavier with each step. She silently sat next to him. He never looked up.

"Hey." She managed to squeak out.

"Hey," he replied. He turned to her and smiled weakly. "You look like hell."

"You're one to talk," she laughed lightly, and handed him a bottle of water.

He grabbed it and took great gulps through cracked lips until it was empty. "Thanks. I think that's the best thing I've ever had."

Juliette took a deep breath. She was ready to get this burden off her chest. "Ronan, I can't even begin to tell you how sorry I am. I don't even know why I said those things. It isn't how I feel about you at all! You are an incredible person, who's only been kind to me. I'm so, so sorry I hurt you."

Ronan didn't respond; he just silently stared at the water.

"I know that there's nothing I can say," she continued, "I hope you can forgive me one day."

Ronan looked at her with his dreamy blue eyes. "Did Pastor Vick tell you that I decided to be a Christian? Like, a real one?"

Juliette's mouth dropped. She hadn't expected this at all.

"Um, no. That's great news!"

Ronan looked back down. "Yeah, I think it is. I don't know what I'm doing, but I'm ready for things to change. Pastor Vick prayed with me for a long time. He's actually an awesome dude."

Neither of them spoke for a few moments. The sun was beginning to peek through the trees, casting a warm glow on their weary bodies.

"I'm sorry for how I treated you, Juliette. If I'm being honest, I was hoping that we would hook up last night, that you'd let your guard down. That sounds terrible no matter how I say it. I want you to know, though, that my feelings for you are real. I wanted to be close to you, not just bone," he gave her a sideways smile. "That seems like a lifetime ago now. I realize now how selfish I've been. You deserve better than that. I've been a jackass to just about everyone I know. You, Mike, Todd, Samantha, more people than I can count. I know I can change, but I've got a lot of work to do."

Juliette took his words in slowly. "I'll forgive you if you forgive me?"

"Deal," he responded. The sat together quietly, breathing in the cool morning air. Ronan broke the silence. "So where do we go from here?"

Juliette cleared her throat. As much as she wanted a relationship with Ronan, it wouldn't be right, for either of them. "I'm thinking about leaving."

Ronan raised his eyebrows.

"There's this short-term missions school in Washington state that my Dad said he'd pay for. I think I'm going to do it. I need a change."

"Wow," Ronan responded flatly. He stared into the water wordlessly. After a few moments he started nodding. "Yeah. You should go for it."

"I leave in three weeks," Juliette said quietly.

"Damn," Ronan spurted out. "I mean, darn. Sorry."

"Don't apologize for everything, Richland." Juliette laughed and punched him lightly on the shoulder.

He cleared his throat. "I think it's great. Truly. I'm going to miss you, though." That familiar tenderness was back in voice.

177

"I'll miss you, too," she smiled back.

"Don't go falling in love with some West-coast surfer boy."

She chuckled. "Okay I'll try not to. Actually, I think I'll stay away from boys for a while. You all are nothing but trouble."

"Can't argue with that."

Juliette rose to her feet. "Come grab a coffee with me. My treat." She offered him her hand.

"I'll take you up on it. I am officially broke for a while," he said as he took her hand and rose. He stumbled a bit as he stood, and grabbed onto Juliette's shoulders for support.

She raised her eyebrows. "You good?"

He squeezed his eyes shut. "Yep, just give me a second."

After a few moments he stood tall, "Okay, ready."

Juliette stared at him, eyebrows still knit in worry.

Ronan gave her a reassuring smile. "I'm fine, Jewels. Just don't ask about it." He gave her shoulders a little squeeze.

Even with the bags under his eyes and his cracked lips, her stomach flipped when he stood next to her. It was a good thing she was leaving. This mess of a boy had stolen her whole heart. As she walked with him to their cars, she breathed in a sigh of relief, along with a pinch of heartache.

Chapter 43

Juliette

A week before her departure as she was sitting on the floor of her room packing, Juliette got a call from Lois. She stared at the phone indignantly, deciding if she wanted anymore drama in her life. She took a deep breath, and exhaled through pursed lips.

"Yes?"

"Hey girl. Can we talk?"

"Isn't that what we're doing?" Juliette snipped. She didn't bother hiding her bitterness, Lois didn't deserve it.

Lois sighed on the other end. "I just found out you're leaving. I wish you would have told me."

"We aren't exactly on speaking terms, Lois."

"I really need to see you. I need to say some stuff. In person."

"Fine. You can come over. I'm in my room packing."

"Be there in ten," Lois said as she hung up.

Juliette carefully put her phone down and stared at the ceiling. "God, I want to snap this girl's neck. Please give me a few extra ounces of patience today."

She didn't look up when Lois walked in and sat on the edge of her bed. She continued to roll t-shirts and stuff them in her suitcase forcefully.

"I'm sorry," Lois finally said after moments of thick silence.

Juliette squeezed her eyes shut, forbidding herself to cry.

"I have been a really sucky friend. I've been jealous of you for a while, and I didn't want to admit it. You're just always so perfect and cute and good at everything. I let it make me bitter. Then when you started dating Todd, who I've liked since kindergarten, it really started to fester."

Juliette angrily threw a pair of socks into her suitcase and turned to face Lois. "You *never* told me you liked Todd. I didn't do anything to you."

"You're right. You didn't. You've been a great friend. I made a complete ass out of myself. I'm so sorry." Lois buried her face in her hands and starting sobbing. "Please forgive me."

Juliette's resolve melted and she jumped up to hug Lois. She cradled her head and kissed the top of her head.

"Okay, hush. I forgive you. Just quit being an 'ass.' I've got a lot of stuff I'm dying to tell you." She stepped back as Lois wiped snot and tears from her face. "And there are a lot of questions I need to ask," she said a little more firmly.

Lois took a deep breath. "I'm ready."

The girls chatted for several hours as Lois helped Juliette pack.

"So, nothing is going on with you and Ronan now?"

"Well, we're friends," Juliette said as she thumbed through the sun dresses in her closet, wondering what the weather would be like in Lynden, Washington this time of year. "There's no point in starting anything else right now. He's leaving, I'm leaving. Maybe we'll just drift apart."

"I think that's sad. You two seemed like you had a real connection."

"Yeah, we do. I want to give him time to get his life together, though. He doesn't need to worry about me right now."

"You're not going to be able to stop him from thinking about you. He looks like a love-sick puppy whenever you two are together. I guess this will be a good test though. There's plenty of chicks to distract him where he's going."

Juliette winced at that last sentence. "Yeah. I guess time will tell."

Chapter 44

Ronan

RONAN SAT BACK ON HIS DORM BED and huffed at his phone. Despite a full day of classes followed by three hours of swim practice, he couldn't relax. Some of the guys from the swim team had invited him out, but he knew from experience with them that it would be a late night, doing a lot of things that he wasn't interested in anymore. It was no fun now that he was the 'sober guy.' He had been in Texas nearly four months and hadn't truly connected with anyone. He had tried joining some on-campus Christian clubs, but most of the members were girls who apparently thought he made great husband material. He missed hanging out with Vick and Dre', who he had spent most of the summer with. Being surrounded by people he didn't care about left him in a pit of suffocating loneliness, and all he could think about as he lay in bed was a sweet girl with chocolate brown eyes, and a butt to kill for.

Juliette was somewhere in Cambodia, or at least that's where she had been the last time they spoke. As much as he prayed about it, there was a constant gnawing prickle in the pit of his stomach. What if she had been kidnapped? A tiny blonde had no business traipsing around the world like this. When he had said this to her before she left, she laughed it off and assured him their team leader was an experienced missionary. He stared at a picture of them now on her Instagram feed, standing at the foot of some glorious mountain. She had neglected to mention that he looked like a Korean pop-star in his mid-twenties.

Probably looking for a wife.

He groaned. This girl was giving him an ulcer. He brushed the screen off angrily and hit favorites on his contacts list. He needed to talk to someone before he lost his mind completely.

"What's up, kid?"

"Hey, Vick. Sorry to bother you again." Ronan could hear the strain in his own voice.

"Ronan, you are never a bother. I'm just coming back from a run. I miss having you as my running partner! How's life in Texas?"

"I don't know, man. It's tough," Ronan said as he laid back in his bed and ran his fingers through his thick dark hair.

"Talk to me," Vick replied. He was an easy outlet, Ronan never felt like he was annoying him. Vick never made him feel weak or weird for having emotions. He had become Ronan's closest friend in the last few months, especially with Juliette so busy and so difficult to get a hold of.

Ronan swallowed hard. "Have you talked to my brother lately? He won't answer my texts. I don't know what's going on with him."

"I've tried checking in on him a few times, but he's never home. I did see him when I was getting gas last week, though. I'll be honest, Ronan, he didn't look great."

"Yeah I figured as much." Guilt and worry pulsated through his veins, making it hard to breathe.

"Is that what's bugging you?" Vick asked.

"Well, yeah. And I haven't heard from Juliette in a while."

"I wouldn't worry about that, Ronan. I hear they keep them pretty busy on those mission trips."

"Maybe. Or she's forgotten about me."

Vick laughed on the other end. "You haven't seen her in five months. Are you still pining for her that hard?"

"I don't know. I really care about her." He pressed his fingers into his eyes, forcing the tears to stay in. "Vick, I think I need to come home."

There was silence on the other end.

"Vick? You still there?"

"I'm here. Just thinking. Do you want to come home for Mike, or for Juliette?"

"For both. I feel like I'm not supposed to be here. I'm spending all my time worrying. I thought I couldn't wait to get out of there, and now I'm counting down the days until Christmas break. I don't think I can bring myself to come back again. I guess I just wanted to see what you thought about it."

"Well, it might be a good idea to come home for your brother's sake. I don't know what will happen with Juliette, but I wish you the best. Personally, I would love your help with the youth group."

"So I'm not crazy for giving this scholarship up? This is a huge opportunity that God gave me here."

"Well, this was always your dream, but it wasn't necessarily God's plan for you. Maybe that's why you're feeling so unsettled. Just pray about it until you've got some peace. I'll be praying for you too, brother. Now, tell me about that assignment you were stressing over. How'd you do?"

They talked for a while about his classes, which he had miraculously done well in. He hung up the phone feeling genuine relief. He had asked for Vick's opinion, but it was more like permission. Having someone to call for advice had made such a difference in his life. Mike and Juliette were two major reasons to come home, but Pastor Vick was a huge reason as well. Now that he had come to terms with the fact that he was leaving, a massive weight lifted from his chest and he settled in to get the first good night's sleep he had had in months.

Chapter 45
Juliette

JULIETTE WOKE UP with enough flurries in her stomach to rival the snow falling against her window. She had prepared endlessly for today. She had rehearsed what she wanted to say a million different ways, but now that the day had come, she was petrified.

She turned on her side and watched the flakes slowly make their way to the earth below.

Ronan is coming home today.

The thought made the flurries rise to her chest, so she sat up and hugged her knees.

Ronan had been on his own journey. Pastor Vick gushed at church about how proud he was of Ronan's spiritual growth. Apparently, they talked regularly, a fact that had made Juliette more than a little jealous. Keeping in touch had proven to be difficult. His class and swim schedule consumed nearly every moment of his day, while she was busy discovering the world. When they were able to speak, it was never enough. There were so many things that she wanted to share with him.

The last six months had been the most meaningful in her life. She'd grown more independent and confident than she ever could have imagined. She always saw herself as a just small-town American girl, but now she had helped build a school in Nepal, held snotty nosed orphans, and wept with mothers who had lost their children to diseases she had never even heard of. She had slept on concrete, felt real hunger for the first time, and had gone days without showering. Even though it had only been a few months, her insight into the rest of the world had cracked open. She was not the same Juliette.

When she hugged him goodbye at the airport before her departure, she wondered if it was possible to move on. It wasn't. Even though her days were long and full, as soon as she laid her head down at night and closed her eyes, she would see that tall boy with crystal blue eyes looking back at her. She made a big decision once she had arrived home two weeks ago, she was going to tell him how she felt.

The day dragged on painfully. Her trepidation grew with every passing hour. She kept herself busy by rearranging her closet, playing Lego with Markus, even cleaning the kitchen, but her anxiety grew nonetheless. She had tried calling Lois, whose constant chatter would prevent any dark thoughts. Unfortunately, she was busy Christmas shopping with Todd, and Juliette refused to be the awkward third wheel. They had begun dating a few months earlier, something that Juliette was both thrilled with and horrified by.

Ronan texted her a few days ago that his plane would land at 4pm, but who knew if he would even want to see her? As little as they had spoken over the last six months, it was possible that he even had a girlfriend. The thought twisted in her side like a knife, so she tried to keep it at bay.

At 4:07 pm she got a text from him "Just landed. Do you want to come over tonight? It would be nice to catch up."

187

"Sure!" Juliette responded and flew into action. She had bought a new outfit specifically for this occasion; a honey-colored blouse with tulip sleeves, embroidered skinny jeans and rose-colored ankle boots. She had even gotten a cute shoulder-length hair cut and mastered styling it with waves. She constantly checked her phone for an update. It seemed an eternity until she got his simple text "home."

Well there's no reading into that, she sighed. It was now or never.

"I'll be over soon," she texted back.

Ten minutes later, she was pulling into his driveway. She suddenly wished she had driven a little slower. Now that the moment was here, she was physically shaking.

When Ronan answered the door, all of her anxieties melted away. Somehow, he had gotten even better looking. He now had a deep, rich tan which set his blue eyes blazing.

"About time! Come in. Let me take your coat."

He pulled her pink pea coat off and threw it to the side before she could answer. He then scooped her into a warm hug. She could have stayed there all night, breathing in that familiar scent of Irish Springs. She lingered longer than she should have. Ronan didn't pull away either, but buried his face in her hair and inhaled deeply.

"God, I missed you," he said under his breath.

She felt her knees weaken. *This must be a good sign.*

He then quickly pulled away, but Juliette could see a dark red in his brown cheeks. She smiled.

"I missed you too, Ronan."

He cocked his head and stared at her until she felt uncomfortable. "You cut your hair."

"Oh, yeah. I did." She touched the ends, suddenly self-conscious. "Is it bad?"

"No!" He reached out and gently ran his fingers through a strand, brushing her cheek softly. Her heart stopped. "You look really pretty."

His hand dropped suddenly, and he cleared his throat.

"I got some Chinese take-out if you're hungry. I thought Mike would be here, but he's out."

"Yeah, sure, that would be great." She felt a little relieved. The air was getting thick between them.

They moved to the kitchen and Ronan dished out their plates. They sat in the living room and laughed and ate together, doing their best to catch up on the time they had spent apart. Juliette carefully watched him and listened as he told stories. He neglected to mention any girls.

Good sign.

He wasn't, however, his old flirtatious self, and had purposefully chosen a spot on the furthest corner of the opposite couch.

Bad sign.

If he was at all interested in her, he was doing a pretty good job of hiding it. She lost track of time while she was sleuthing, and before she knew it, it was 10 pm.

"I didn't realize how late it was! I promised mom I'd help wrap some presents tonight. I should go."

"Yeah, of course. We'll catch up more tomorrow," Ronan said ruefully.

Juliette slowly walked to the door, and Ronan behind followed silently. She was vacillating on what to do. She knew herself well enough to know that if she let this chance pass, she'd let his whole winter break go by without saying anything.

She stopped herself before she got her coat.

You have to do to this - now!

She took a deep breath, turned, and said, "Ronan-"

"Juliette," he said at the same time.

They grinned at each other and said, "You first," simultaneously.

"Jinx! That means you go," he said pointing at her.

"I don't think that's how jinx works, but okay." She squeezed her eyes shut and summoned all her courage. "Ronan, I love you."

Silence followed. She opened her eyes but found his face to be unreadable.

Might as well keep going at this point.

"I know you're leaving in a couple of weeks and we won't see each other again for months, but I think maybe we should try and see what it's like to be together."

She lost her nerve suddenly. He stared at her, wide-eyed and speechless.

Say something, you stupid boy!

"I know I rejected before, but I wasn't ready then, and you probably weren't either. I'm ready now. I want to be with you, if you still care about me."

He kept staring, as motionless as a statue. Horror overcame her as she realized she had likely just made a fool of herself. Hot tears threatened the rims of her eyes.

Say something. Anything! She pleaded mentally, but he didn't.

"Ronan-" she said desperately, just as he took a broad step toward her.

Without saying a word, he cupped her face in his hands and lifted it to his. He pressed his forehead against hers and stared into her very soul as he slowly, tantalizingly, brushed his lips against hers. He kissed her gently at first, tenderly caressing her lips until she stepped into him and wrapped her hands around his waist, spreading her fingers over the strong muscles of his back, pulling him closer. He countered by putting one arm around her back and tangling his other hand in her hair. He kissed her deeper and deeper, exploring her with the tip of his tongue. He was so much larger and stronger than she was, he engulfed her tiny frame. It was intoxicating. The moment she thought she might collapse upon herself, he pulled away and kissed her forehead. He traced her back with trembling fingers and settled on the small of her waist. She had never felt more vulnerable, or more safe.

"Do you know how long I've wanted to do that?" He whispered, his lips brushing her baby hairs.

She was stupefied, unable to respond. She rested her head against his chest and let his heart pound against her cheek. They stood silent and breathless.

"I'm not going back to Texas, Jewels."

She pulled away, ready to protest, but he put his finger to her lips before she had a chance.

"Before you say anything, I'm not quitting college. I'll be going to State University of New York. They have a great swim team, and it's only a two-hour drive. I couldn't stand it in Texas another minute. Mike isn't doing well. I'm worried about him. He needs me here, but mostly, I need you."

"Ronan, isn't this something you'll regret?"

"The only thing I'll regret is if I let you get away," he said with a soft smile. "Being away from you was torture. I was worried about you every second. Worried you would get hurt, worried you'd get kidnapped, worried you'd forget about me, worried you would find someone else." He stopped suddenly, his eyes misty. "I love you so much, you crazy little woman. I just want to be with you. You're right, I wasn't ready before. But I am now. I will abide by every rule and boundary you give me." He looked at her worried. "Maybe I should have asked about that before I kissed you."

She giggled. "Obviously I didn't mind, silly."

"Phew. Anyway, I swear I will treat you like a queen."

A warm glow spread in her chest. "Don't you mean like a Princess?"

He chuckled and leaned into her again. "Yes, like a Princess. My Princess."

He slowly kissed her forehead and cheeks, finishing with a tender kiss on the tip of her nose before pulling her into a close hug. She wrapped her arms around his neck and nestled into his solid chest. She smiled when she realized how perfectly they fit together, like missing puzzle pieces. She ran her fingers through his dark hair, kissed his cheek, and whispered into his ear, "Welcome home."

"O daughters of Jerusalem, I adjure you: do not awaken love until it is ready."

- Song of Solomon 8:4

ABOUT THE AUTHOR

Jenny Taylor is a Christian first, a wife second, a mother third, and a nurse fourth. She is passionate about all of these. She grew up as a missionary/preacher's kid and spent the first 9 years of her life in Germany. She is now married with two precious daughters and teaches full time in a nursing program in Delaware.

Made in the USA
Middletown, DE
07 May 2020